Lost Journals of Black Gold

आबनूस सोना

Shadow Reign Chronicles Vol. 1

Samantha Perkins

To Tiffanie Kee'ra,

Enjoy!

Samantha Perkins

Copyright © 2013 Samantha Perkins

All rights reserved.

ISBN: 1494449269
ISBN 13: 9781494449261
Library of Congress Control Number: 2013922891
CreateSpace Independent Publishing Platform
North Charleston, South Carolina

Dedications and Acknowledgments

This novel is dedicated to community organizers and leaders throughout the world—those seen and unseen. Just know that your service to humanity never goes unnoticed by the Most High.

Special acknowledgment goes to Ultra Translate LLC for providing translation of English words and phrases into Hindi for this novel. For over ten years, this company has provided certified human translation in place of machine translation.

Finally, thank you to my readers: enjoy this new series!

    Samantha Arlene Perkins समंथा अर्लेने पर्किस

Prologue/ Importance of Language

The story and characters in this novel are fictitious in nature with the exception of Dr. Samarjit Jana. He is a public health scientist who organized a peer educator team among sex workers of the area of Sonagachi—the largest red-light district in Kolkata, West Bengal, India. The peer educator team formed in 1992 for the main purpose of HIV intervention research study. The research team learned of other critical issues among the prostitutes, such as education for their children and use of contraceptives. In 1995 Dr. Jana and twelve sex workers formed the Durbar Mahila Samanwaya Committee. Since its inception the organization's main projects are advocating sex worker's rights, antihuman trafficking, and HIV prevention. The work of Dr. Jana and his team has lowered the HIV infections of people in the red-light district of Kolkata and has educated the people in this world to seek better health practices for themselves.

In researching India, I felt it was important to illustrate the rich culture of the people. The challenge for me lay in illustrating the many languages and dialects used based on the region where the people reside. A few of my central characters are from the eastern region of India. In this region the people speak predominantly Bengali but also various dialects from their native mother tongue. In India over seven hundred languages are spoken, and many phrases and words vary based on the region of the people. However, India's *agreed* national language is Hindi. There are Hindu temples all over India, including the location where the novel mainly takes place—Kolkata, West Bengal, India. To demonstrate appreciation for both the West and East, I thought it best to illustrate the more dominate languages of both the United States and India. The specific focus on Hindi and English should not convey to readers that I am purposely removing substance and relevance from indigenous practiced customs, cultures, and dialects spoken in India or the United States.

Table of Contents

Chapters अध्याय

Dedications and Acknowledgments	iii
Prologue/Importance of Language	v
One: Relocation Assignment—दूसरे जगह का कार्यभार	1
Two: Chopping Block—तलवार की धार	17
Three: Hookah Pipes & Dinner Play—हुक्का का पाइप एवं रात्रिभोज का मंचन	29
Four: Being a Khan—खान होने के कारण	47
Five: Shadow Reign or Aisha Benson?—छद्मनाम या आइसा बेंसन?	55
Six: The World's Oldest Profession—दुनिया का सबसे पुराना पेशा	61
Seven: Up, Up, and Away—निर्भय होकर आगे बढ़ो	69
Eight: Welcome to Kolkata—कोलकाता में आपका स्वागत है	75

Nine: The Tourist Experience—पर्यटक का अनुभव 89

Ten: The Red-Light District—वेश्यावृति प्रभावति जलि 97

Eleven: Lost Journals—गुम हो चुकी पत्रिकाएँ 107

Twelve: Who Do You Think You Are? A Hero?—
खुद को क्या समझते हैं? एक नायक? 113

Thirteen: This Is Our Life—यह हमारा जीवन है 123

Fourteen: Diwali, Festival of Lights—ज्योति पर्व दीपावली 141

Fifteen: Black Gold—आबनूस सोना 149

Sixteen: Assignment Completed—नियत कार्य पूरा हो गया 169

About the Author—लेखक के बारे में 177

Relocation Assignment
दूसरे जगह का कार्यभार

"I don't get you." Aisha was lying on her stomach on the bed, smoking a Newport cigarette, and looking at her boyfriend kneeling down in prayer.

"What you don't get is that you're supposed to be praying with me." Majid interrupted his own prayer session to respond to her. His prayer mat had a woven compass on it, and his body was positioned facing Mecca.

"I'm not a practicing Muslim, remember?" Aisha rolled her eyes, inhaled her cigarette, and rolled over onto her back to look up at the ceiling. "I don't get why you shower and immediately kneel down to prayer right after we make love. Are you purging your guilt toward Allah because of my ethnicity or because you should be with a woman who honors chastity?" Aisha defiantly asked.

Majid ignored her comments long enough to complete his prayer. He removed his kufi, as he only wore it when praying, and placed it in their dresser drawer. Then he rolled up the prayer mat and stood it up on the wall in their closet. His brown eyes looked over at Aisha, who was puffing on her cigarette, looking up at the ceiling. Brushing her hair with his hands, he sat down on the bed. "Well, Aisha, I can only marry a Muslim woman. You do realize this, correct?" Majid continued, "As far as your ethnicity, we've been in a relationship way too long to keep going over this. You respect my family's home, you respect our culture, and when we are in mosque, you practice. If I were to leave you today, it wouldn't be for you being a black woman or your lack of chastity. I was your first, last, and only."

Majid motioned for Aisha to place the cigarette in his mouth; he exhaled the smoke into her mouth as they shared a passionate kiss. He said, "I want you to quit; but it is kind of sexy to see you puffing on it. I realize it was me who got you into smoking in the first place; so it's basically my fault." He licked the side of her neck to distract her and snatched the cigarette out of her hand. He walked into the bathroom and flushed the butt down the toilet. "Smoking is the problem. So no more about ethnicity, understood? Besides, you know my culture. Our weddings last for days; not sure if you could hang," Majid said jokingly while walking into their kitchen to prepare dinner.

The two of them had been in a relationship for nine years. Aisha met Majid in her senior year of college at the age of twenty-one. She had accidentally bumped into him while jogging in East Rock Park before she went to class on the Yale campus. Aisha was an English major aspiring to become a journalist after graduation. The attraction was instant; Majid was a biochemistry professor at the University of Connecticut, and he was in town for a teachers' convention. That weekend they were only separate from one another when she was in class or when he had seminars to attend. They exchanged numbers and home addresses. Nine years had since passed, and for the past year they had been living in their condo in West Hartford, Connecticut. Majid was thirty-six, six years her senior.

"Are you preparing the ilish?" Aisha asked, sliding on her robe to join Majid in the kitchen. She ran up behind him and placed her hands in his front pockets.

"Of course. You're gonna make the rice, right?" Majid asked, taking the fish out of the freezer.

Aisha nodded her head. "I'm so glad that when your mom went to Dhaka she brought back the fish. It is so good." She went inside of their pantry to get out the rice. "You'll make the fish the Bengali way, and I'll prepare the rice the Gullah way," Aisha said.

"Gullah?" Majid asked, curious.

"Yeah, my people are from the low country region of the US: South Carolina. I explained this to you years ago." Aisha got out a pot, placed water in it, and set it on the stove.

"I love soul food rice," Majid said and went behind her to kiss her neck.

"Soul food rice? Whatever, man." Aisha moaned as he kissed and licked the back of her neck, which he knew was her spot. "So do we plan on preparing dinner right now, or are we ready to go back into the bedroom?" She couldn't resist his kisses any longer and turned around to face him.

He picked her up and placed her on the kitchen counter. "Who needs to go back into the bedroom?" Majid asked and spread Aisha's legs...

The pair enjoyed eating their dinner at the kitchen table in silence—how Majid preferred it. He enjoyed the moments of tasting every morsel of his food until it went down his throat. When Majid was finished, he stacked his plates, one on top of the other, put his utensils on last, and pushed away from the table to indicate to Aisha he was done. Aisha just finished her food and took his dirty dishes into the kitchen and placed them into the dishwasher; she went back to the kitchen table to retrieve hers and put them in the dishwasher as well. Majid very rarely helped clean up after dinner; he believed it was women's work, and Aisha did not mind. She grew up in quite a traditional Muslim household. Majid had very similar qualities to her father. Both men believed in the traditional roles of males and females in the household. Majid did believe in preparing dinner with Aisha, whereas her father never did.

Her parents had been married for twenty-five years and explained to Aisha and Majid one day that the key to their marriage was keeping the roles simple between husband and wife. "Women need direction, and men are to provide that," Aisha's father had said, looking over to his wife. "She has birthed three of my children and raised them while I worked hard for my family. Khadijah is a good woman. She taught Aisha to be respectful of others, nurturing, and not combative; my daughter's attitude is not what you would find in most American women of today's times."

Majid went into the sun-room of their condo and sat down on the sofa. He picked up a book and started to read. Aisha wiped down the kitchen table, cleaned the counter, and started the dishwasher. "Hey, honey, looks like the garbage is ready to be taken out." Aisha put the top down on the garbage, walked into the sun-room, and sat next to her man.

"I'll take it out before I head to bed tonight," Majid said, turning the pages of his book. Aisha placed her head on his shoulders. Whenever she did this, it indicated to him that she needed his advice. "What's on your mind, love?" Majid asked.

She removed her shoes and lay on the sofa, placing her head on his lap. "My boss, Larry, needs a journalist to go overseas for a story. People are saying in the office that he may ask me if I would be interested." Aisha paused for a reaction.

Majid placed his hand on his chin and rubbed his goatee. "Where does he want a journalist to go?" he asked her, his stare focused toward a distant place.

"Well, there is a rumor going around the office that he wants someone who can get their hands on a good story in Mumbai," she explained, tracing her fingers over his face.

Majid stood at five feet eleven inches, with coarse, textured, black hair that he kept in a Caesar hair cut. His facial features were a mixture of African and Asian. He had an athletic toned body: more of a basketball player type than the body mass of a football player. His complexion had a dark brown, reddish undertone, and his deep chocolate eyes were Asiatic in form. Aisha loved the shape and intensity in his eyes; it seemed as if they saw deep into her soul every time he looked at her. "India? The flight is long; you know how impatient you are, right? Not sure if this would be the right assignment for you." Majid looked down at her and rubbed her cheek gently.

"Oh, come on, honey." Aisha sat up and looked him in the eyes. "I have never been out of the country on assignment. This is my chance to prove myself. I am ready. Just wanted to see how you would feel about it." She looked away, playing with her hands in her lap.

"How long would this journalist be in India?" Majid asked sternly.

"It sounded like a month." Aisha closed her eyes.

Majid shook his head and laughed. "You in a foreign country for a month by yourself? I'm not in love with this idea, honey. What do you know about Mumbai? I'm concerned about your safety there; do you have any girlfriends that live in Mumbai?" Majid asked.

Aisha contemplated the question. "Chandi's mother and father live there. If I remember correctly, she goes there once a year during the fall season to visit them," Aisha said, proud of herself that she had a solid answer for his question.

"If you could be there when Chandi is there, I would feel comfortable with you going. India is not America. In some areas you're going to see people in conditions that you would have never thought they'd be in. My advice is to stay in South Mumbai: in the city area. You stay there, and you'll get more of an American experience." Majid got up and walked into their bedroom. He took out of the closet a pair of black dress pants, some black dress shoes, and a collared navy blue shirt.

Aisha followed behind him and jumped on the bed. "Preparing your clothes for work tomorrow?" She watched.

Majid ignored her question. "Let your boss bring up this trip to you first before you go and volunteer yourself. I am not crazy about the idea of you being there without me, but I think this could be an eye-opening experience for you. Black Americans aren't known for traveling outside of the States as much as other groups of people. There is a big world out there, and you'd be surprised how many groups of people follow black music, culture." Majid hung his work clothes on their bedroom door, started the shower, and undressed in the bathroom.

"Well, we black Americans are more than musicians and athletes," Aisha said over the noise of the water current flowing from the shower.

"Right, but that's all those people over there see on TV; so you can go over there and show them something else. I was born here, but my parents did not know much about black Americans. And your family is nothing like what they thought about them. There are a lot of misconceptions and misunderstandings; I'm glad I grew up here. Most of my friends, as you know, are black; most people, especially white people, confuse me for being black anyway." Majid removed his white tank top to reveal his chiseled frame. He pulled off his black work-out pants and dropped his boxers to the bathroom floor.

Aisha went into the bathroom and studied her man's body, looking him up and down. "Oh, you're definitely a brotha," Aisha joked and grabbed his head to kiss him on the lips, then wrapped her arms around his shoulders.

Majid smirked and returned her passionate kisses. He got into the shower and positioned his body underneath the stream of water. He rubbed shampoo into his hands and lathered it on his hair. He moved the shower curtain out of the way to look at Aisha. "You gonna join me?" Majid's teeth were a bright white and were glowing against his dark skin.

"I'd be a fool not to; let me get my shower cap." She undressed, put on the shower cap, and hopped in.

Aisha was at work the next day, sitting in her cubicle, surfing the web. She thought about her conversation with her boyfriend and considered his point of view. Granted, she did not know much about India, but all the more reason to go. How exciting it would be to see the Taj Mahal in person, even though that would be another plane ride from Mumbai. *But a realistic adventure nonetheless*, Aisha thought. Experience Mumbai's booming city district, possibly tour Bollywood, and, of course, Indian cuisine. She sipped her ginger chai tea, thinking of the adventure she could possibly have ahead.

"Hey, girl." Kelsey walked into Aisha's cube and plopped down on her visitor's chair. She crossed her legs and picked up the Rubik's Cube on Aisha's desk. "You still haven't figured this thing out yet?" Kelsey asked, fidgeting with it.

"I pick it up usually to play with it whenever I feel like I'm falling asleep," Aisha responded, continuing to surf the web.

"Your man is still keeping you up all hours of the night?" Kelsey joked. Aisha did not respond but smiled at her co-worker and returned to her computer screen. "So when is he going to get around to proposing to you? You all have been together forever." Kelsey was focused on the cube.

"He's a black man. You know they're allergic to marriage. Just joking. I don't know. I guess he will know when the time is right. I don't bother him about it," Aisha confessed.

"I thought he was Indian," Kelsey said, fixated on the cube.

"He's Bengali, but you know what I mean," Aisha responded.

"There! I did it!" Kelsey placed the cube back on Aisha's desk and looked proudly at her accomplishment of solving the 3D puzzle.

"Oh, you did this, did you?" Aisha said, holding the puzzle up in amazement. Kelsey grinned from ear to ear. Aisha sarcastically laughed and moved the squares around on the cube until it was in a confused puzzle again.

"Are you nuts? You should have at least waited for me to take a picture of it so that I could put it on Facebook." She made a pouty face.

"I told you it's my way of staying awake. Besides, I solved that thing two weeks ago." Aisha gently pushed her friend, who looked dumbfounded.

"Oh, you had me thinking you never got it," Kelsey said.

"Yeah, I know." Aisha patted her sweater pockets, took out a Newport, and made a smoking gesture toward Kelsey, signaling a cig break.

"Let's go." Kelsey led the way outside.

"How's that story going with the inventor of what again?" Aisha asked, lighting up.

Kelsey grunted. "The inventor of the mechanical makeup remover; geez, don't get me started. The guy at times is hard to reach, and since we are giving him free publicity and all, I tried it. It made my face look like the Joker's," Kelsey said.

Aisha laughed. "What? Sounds like it doesn't work!"

Kelsey nodded her head. "It's one of those inventions you see on infomercials," she began.

The two said in unison, "But wait! There's more!" Kelsey and Aisha laughed.

"So what's included when people buy it?" Aisha asked.

"They can get a travel-size mirror with a small Caboodles case in leopard print or pink," Kelsey said.

"Cool, so I get to look at the results of the mechanical makeup remover thanks to the included compact mirror to see how much money I wasted on that crap when my face looks like the Joker's. Awesome, girlfriend." Aisha gave Kelsey a high five.

"I don't even know how our paper stays afloat sometimes, let alone send one person every year to a far-off destination in search of an eye-awakening story," Kelsey said. The two finished their cigarettes and began to head back to the office.

"Good point. Well, you know Jared's team always gets praised for their story coverages, and we have to admit they are good; true journalism!" Aisha exclaimed, going through the double glass doors first, while Kelsey caught it behind her.

"That story covered on the teachers' budget cut was very enlightening and a tearjerker when he got real gut-wrenching testimony from a few teachers. I never knew how unappreciated their efforts were," Kelsey concluded.

The two of them got back into the office, and Kelsey walked Aisha back to her desk. The two women small-talked for a bit until Larry Goldstein, their boss, walked into Aisha's cubicle. Larry was in his midfifties, of a stocky build, and around five feet six inches. He had liver spots on his neck and face, and thick, black eyebrows formed a monobrow over his eyes. He hung his hand over the cubicle wall and looked at Kelsey and Aisha talking.

Larry cleared his throat. "Ms. Benson, I'd like to see you in my office right away." Larry left the cubicle area and walked in the direction of his office.

Kelsey shrugged her shoulders at Aisha, who wore a confused stare. "I can't think of anything I did wrong. Don't know why I got called to the principal's office," she said to Kelsey and giggled.

Patina Smith, whose cubicle was in front of Aisha's, heard everything and decided to poke her head over the cubicle wall. "Well, you ladies have been talking the majority of the morning, and this is not happy hour, ladies. This is a place of business." Kelsey and Aisha looked at each other and rolled their eyes. Patina continued, "As of late, when you all are not talking, you're going on smoke breaks, so I've noticed. Perhaps Larry needs to fill you in on how to conduct yourselves in the workplace." Patina grinned and slowly sat back down in her office chair and turned her head toward her computer.

"Just go and see what Goldstein wants, and fill me in later," Kelsey said to Aisha. Aisha showed signs of concern and grimaced. "Hey, text me if you need to after your meeting with him, OK?" Kelsey left Aisha's cubicle.

As Kelsey walked by Patina's cube, she noticed Patina's lunch and her fork lying close to the edge of Patina's desk. Kelsey pushed Patina's fork off of her desk. Patina always brought her own food as well as utensils from home, and everyone in the vicinity heard the metal fork hit the ground. "Oops! I guess me walking by your desk so fast blew your fork off your plate. My bad, Patina." Kelsey turned back around and raised an eyebrow at another co-worker who saw exactly what Kelsey did,

"You're so bad," Marissa whispered. Kelsey smiled and continued to walk away.

Aisha stood up from her desk and walked toward her boss's office. Larry's office was situated toward the back of the floor. She noticed Jared Livingston sitting in his cubicle. As Aisha walked by him, she noticed his scathing appearance as he looked directly at her. Aisha was taken aback by his facial expression, and her eyes widened, but she kept walking toward Goldstein's office. Larry's office door was slightly ajar and she knocked on the door.

"Benson! Come on in. Have a seat." Larry placed his finger up, motioning for her to wait a minute while he finished typing on his computer. "Benson, never forget in this business there is always someone to answer to. You have me, and I have Julia Weathers. Ah, there we go." Larry finished typing. He placed the keyboard in the desk tray and turned his attention toward Aisha. "Benson, you have been with *Hartford Journal* for how long now?" Larry got up from his chair and rubbed his chin and looked out of his window.

Aisha crossed her legs and slightly bobbed the top leg up and down, placing her hands on her knee. "I've been with the paper for five years, sir," Aisha said confidently.

Larry turned back to her. "That's right. We've placed you on a couple of assignments, locally only though, and then you have the stories you choose to write about. Tell me, what are your aspirations with the paper, Benson?" Larry looked intently at her, waiting for her response.

"Well, honestly, sir, I believe I am one of your most talented journalists. I just need the right story to prove I can be just as credible as, let's say, Jared Livingston." Aisha matched his stare and spoke sternly.

Larry shrugged his shoulders and placed his arms behind his back. "Well, Aisha, I am not going to beat around the bush any further. We have an assignment that needs someone who is of a certain talent." Larry sat back down in his chair.

Aisha swallowed hard, and her eyes beamed. "Um, sir, if you do not mind, I'll interject here. I heard something about a journalist going to Mumbai...?" Aisha rubbed her hands together as she spoke.

"Not quite. No offense, Benson, but if it was in the budget here for a journalist to go to Mumbai—and depending on the story—we would have asked Jared Livingston. No, this is a unique and quirky sort of assignment. Unique and quirky is right up your alley. Julia and I went over your file and the work you've produced. You tend to work on assignments that have a quirky and unique element to them. Like, for instance, that story you did back in 2012 with the nationally renowned clairvoyant on an earthly cosmic paradigm shift; that takes talent. You almost had me believing it, and Julia got a nice laugh out of it. In fact, all of our executives got a chuckle out of it." Larry started laughing.

Aisha looked puzzled, as she had not written the article to be taken as humorous. Larry stopped laughing after he noticed she had a confused expression on her face.

"Hmm; OK. Listen: there is a story to be told in Kolkata. So, the rumor was right about India, but not the correct state or city. Kolkata is located in West Bengal." Larry took out his tablet and thumbed through his e-mails. "Look here." Larry handed the tablet to Aisha.

Aisha saw a photo with crowds of people walking on the streets of Kolkata, and she specifically noticed alleyways pierced with red light. "OK, what am I looking at?" Aisha handed him back the tablet.

"You're looking at a story. I cannot send Jared there; this is the red-light district of Kolkata. We need someone who can blend into the crowd, if you know what I mean," Larry said matter-of-factly. "The minute they see Jared, they'll think he's a cop or a john."

"Excuse me?" Aisha felt insulted.

"Listen, you will have the best protection that the consulate can provide you. Basically, the women of that world never let outsiders in. The last time someone from the paper who was of the Euro persuasion went into the world of the red-light district of Kolkata, they confiscated her camera, and she came back with nothing but her memories and one special item."

"OK, so where do I fit into this?" Aisha said.

Larry fidgeted in his chair. "I guess I'm not making myself clear. The red-light district refers to brothels, gentlemen clubs. Make sense now?" Larry said, obviously very uncomfortable with having this conversation with his employee.

"What! Larry, are you kidding? What type of story are you expecting to get out of there that is not right here in America?" Aisha asked, feeling the need to grab her sweater wrap taut across her body and cross her legs tighter.

"We've heard that there are children born into this life, an endless, depressing cycle generation after generation. And I'm telling you we need someone who can get into their world so that we can get that story." Larry, still uncomfortable, looked away from Aisha. "Think of the voice you would create for those children," Larry said, continuing to push his idea.

"Are you sure there are children in these places?" Aisha asked.

"There have been documentaries about this district, but no one has gotten close enough to see if there is more to the stories. My sources, whom I can't share all of the names with you, believe there is a deeper story than just the children." Larry returned to his desk and took out a manila envelope from one of the drawers. He looked at the envelope, removed a framed photo, and paused for a moment. "Here is the special item Lydia managed to bring back."

He handed Aisha a six-by-nine-inch black-and-white photo preserved with a matte finish cover and encased with metal reinforcements on each corner. The photo had definitely been taken many years ago. Aisha inspected the photo and put her hands up to her mouth. "What the...! This woman...how...She looks exactly like me." Aisha was flabbergasted and placed the photo on her thigh.

"The resemblance is uncanny. Lydia, the woman I told you about who went on assignment to Kolkata years ago for the paper, found this photo, I gather, in one of the brothels. This woman has a story, Aisha. She must have some high importance in the redlight district, or she would not have been adorned the way she is in this photo. This is the only evidence Lydia brought back to the States. She kept the photo on her at all times before handing it in to the consulate. When the local women noticed the photograph was missing, they immediately accused Lydia of stealing it and kicked her out of their homes and stole her camera. Good thing she handed in that photo to the consulate shortly after she found it," Larry sat back down, holding his hand out to get the photo back from Aisha.

"At the time the photo was taken," said Larry, "this woman had to be around thirty years of age, and she is African American. She was a journalist. We think she remained in India by her own will, since there was no story about her being kidnapped. Her family here in the States never communicated with the consulate and never reported her whereabouts to the media. She went on assignment twenty years ago with another paper that our company merged with late last year. I do not expect you to provide an answer now. Julia is giving you until next Monday to decide. This would be a three-month relocation to Kolkata, West Bengal, all expenses paid: food, hotel, everything. We just ask you to come back with the story. *You* need that story," Larry confessed.

"I have to think about this. You know I have my significant other. Ooh, boy, is he not going to be happy about this." Aisha grabbed her twist-out Afro.

"Oh, I see. You are still dating the Indian professor, right?" Larry asked.

"Yes," Aisha answered hesitantly, not sure how he knew her business like that.

"Kelsey told me years ago at one of our office holiday parties," Larry said nonchalantly. "See, you're turning out to be the perfect person for the assignment already," Larry said, getting up from his desk.

"The perfect person? Because I am dating an Asian man and I look like some woman? How does this make me the perfect person for the assignment?" Aisha followed suit and got up from her seat.

"Well, Ms. Benson, our time is up. Just think about it, and get back to me by e-mail. In between now and Monday, feel free to send me any questions you have about the assignment. I know what we're asking of you is a lot to take in," Larry said as he walked Aisha toward his office door. "Get back to work, Benson. Oh, and don't worry about Patina. Everyone on this floor wanted this assignment and knew I'd ask you." Larry patted her on the back. "Or should I say knew I wanted Shadow Reign on the assignment. It's typical for a journalist to have a pen name, so I've never questioned anyone on my staff about their aliases. But, Benson, you've piqued my curiosity; why Shadow Reign as a fictitious name?" Larry asked her.

Aisha thought about it for a second and responded. "The word *shadow* can be defined as a dark illumination: dark matter illuminated. That's my alter ego, I investigate and report back. Shadow Reign can't stop attracting the unique and quirky stories, as you called my writing earlier," she concluded.

"You have some imagination. I'm hoping you'll get back to me sooner rather than later, Ms. Benson." Larry looked at her curiously and closed his office door behind her.

Chopping Block
तलवार की धार

After work Aisha and Kelsey went around the corner from their office building to T.G.I. Fridays for drinks and much discussion on the politics of their jobs. The ladies ordered their drinks and got right into it. "So tell me what happened with Goldstein," Kelsey said, exhaling the smoke from her Marlboro cigarette.

A smile came across Aisha's face. "I guess the rumors were true. Larry asked me to go on assignment in India." The two women giggled and smiled like teenage girls and slapped hands.

"You are so incredibly lucky. I wish I could have gotten the assignment. I basically knew that was why he called you into the office too, though." Kelsey patted her cigarette into the ashtray to get the ash off.

"How did you know?" Aisha said, taking a Newport out of her purse.

Kelsey smiled. "You know Jared has a thing for me. So he gave me some information if I agreed to go out on a date with him," she concluded.

"Cool. You have got to tell me everything. When I was walking toward Goldstein's office, Jared gave me the most critical look I've ever seen. I didn't know where it came from," Aisha said, lighting her cigarette.

"OK, you asked for it; you want to know everything. Aisha, you have to take this assignment. Your job depends on it." Kelsey inhaled her cigarette and raised her finger, indicating she was not done. "The corporate executives of our company don't understand your writing. They think you're the oddest or weakest link of our paper. And since corporations always look for ways to cut back, they are looking to make some employee cuts this year. Your name was on the chopping block. Long story short: Goldstein fought to keep you employed here once he figured out a way to do so." Kelsey looked into Aisha's eyes, noticing her somber reaction. "Allegedly there is some woman journalist who you resemble. You have an almost an exact replica of her characteristics, so to speak. She worked for a company we acquired last year, and she ended up in India for some reason. I guess she lives in Mumbai." Kelsey shrugged her shoulders and inhaled from her cigarette.

"It's actually Kolkata," Aisha said, still pondering what Kelsey revealed to her. The girls thanked the waitress after receiving their drinks.

"Kolkata? Ugh! Never mind. I would not have wanted this story after all. Haven't heard many nice things about Kolkata." Kelsey looked disgusted.

Aisha grinned. "Excuse me, but whose friend are you? When did you know my name was on the chopping block, Miss Thing?" Aisha asked.

"About a month ago. Listen, I didn't want to say anything to you—yet. It was best for me to wait for Goldstein. You know Larry tells Jared everything, so I'm going to continue to engage Jared for work reasons, of course," Kelsey said, sipping her mojito.

"Oh, please! You know you like Jared too. I don't blame you; he is cute," Aisha said.

"I know." Kelsey's eyes appeared dreamy. "Just take the assignment. The evil corporate sorcerers are using their magic wands and laying off tons of people by the end of this year," Kelsey said.

"Really? Well, who else's neck was up to be hanged?" Aisha asked, sipping her martini.

"Uhh, Patina Smith, Marissa Stringer, Jamal Walton, Antoine Peterson, Chris Santos, and Tameka Green," Kelsey answered.

Aisha envisioned every individual Kelsey rambled off. "Wait a second. That's like every black or Latino person in our department," Aisha said.

Kelsey held up her hands. "Hey, I don't know what the executives are doing, but I have to admit that once Jared told me this info, that was the first thing I thought as well." Kelsey gave an uncomfortable look to Aisha.

"Well, why did Goldstein want to salvage me then?" Aisha asked, puzzled.

"You don't know after all these years? You still don't see it?" Kelsey asked. Aisha looked around. "Oh, goodness," Kelsey continued. "He's sweet on you. Come on, girl. Your articles interviewing clairvoyants, spiritual awakenings? You work for a corporation. You thought those articles were going to give you the respect you deserve at the *Hartford Journal*? Maybe if you wrote an article on the *money gods*, they would have given you admiration. You don't speak their language, boo. You've got to speak corporate journalistic language to stay afloat here," Kelsey reasoned with her.

"Corporate journalistic language. But you don't speak that either. Your articles could be taken to be just as silly as mine and not nearly as substantive," Aisha said.

"Well, I am obviously protected, right? Jared has Goldstein wrapped around his finger. I'm good. Never worry about yours truly." Kelsey batted her blue eyes at Aisha.

"Right," Aisha said, narrowing her brown eyes.

"Trust me: take the assignment. I can't have my partner in crime get tossed out like the morning paper." Kelsey eyed Aisha, nodded, and looked away.

isha came home to find a note Majid had left on the refrigerator door:

> Isha,
> I went to pick up some juice from the store. Will be home soon.
> Majid

Aisha pulled the note off and threw it away after reading it. She went inside the freezer and removed some frozen vegetables to steam cook after her shower. While she was in the shower, she lathered up her Afro in conditioner and stuck her body underneath the water. She kept her head down, thinking of this new opportunity that had her employment with the *Hartford Journal* hanging by a thin thread.

Well, I will have consulate protection, hopefully a nice hotel, good food, still get paid as well. Doesn't sound terribly awful, although Mumbai has a classier reputation, Aisha thought.

After she wrung her hair out and placed it in a bun, she started to wash her body. Aisha heard Majid's footsteps come into their bedroom, which was right off of their bathroom.

"Hey, babe, I got your message!" Aisha shouted out.

Majid did not respond but hurriedly left the room, seeming to leave in as quiet of a manner as possible.

"Babe, you there, or am I hearing things?" Aisha asked out loud and continued to finish cleaning her body. She got out of the shower and placed a couple of two-stranded twists in her hair and covered it with a scarf, allowing her hair to air-dry. She wrapped her robe around her damp body and walked out to their bedroom.

"Oh my God!" Aisha exclaimed. On their bed Majid had left a bunch of red and pink rose petals that made a heart shape. She took one of the petals to her nose and smelled its sweet floral scent. "Babe, you did this for us?" Aisha said and turned around to see Majid standing behind her. He had on black pajama pants and no shirt.

He brought her hand up to his mouth and kissed it. "We haven't had a romantic night in a long time. I used to be romantic, right?" Majid asked, staring intently into Aisha's eyes while picking her up and slowly bringing her down to the bed.

"Umm, yes, in the beginning we had some romantic rendezvous before intercourse, but I don't remember complaining about it," Aisha said, moving her twists to the side to rest her head comfortably on the pillows.

"You're amazing and I love how patient you are with me. I want you to take the assignment. I want you to be happy in your career, and my insecurities should not get in the way of that. I have a wonderful, truly devoted woman. And, let's face it, after nine years we haven't gone anywhere but to each other. Take the assignment, baby girl," Majid said before kissing her neck.

"Uh, wow. I did not think it would be that easy for you to agree with this, but OK, I will," Aisha said, smiling.

Majid got on the bed and lay next to her. "Put your head on my shoulder. I love when you do that," Majid said to her.

Aisha positioned her head on his left shoulder and spread some of the rose petals on his abs.

"How does this moment feel, Isha?" Majid asked.

"Like a huge weight has been lifted off of me. I can't believe you're cool with this," she said.

"No, not that. This moment. You and I together?" Majid asked, looking down at her.

"Oops. Sorry. Honey, looking into your eyes I feel this moment every day. I feel loved, protected, and sexy." She pulled his waist into hers.

"Tomorrow Mel and I are going to hang out. Tonya, his wife, will be there too. You know he is my oldest friend. Mel moved to Atlanta after school, but since he's in town, I wanted you to meet him and his wife," Majid said.

"Cool. Where are we going to go?" Aisha asked, tracing the petals on Majid's abs.

"Mel and I were going to initially make this a guy's night out, so we decided to stick with the plan of going to a hookah bar. When he told me Tonya was in town as well, I had to of course brag about my lady, so we're meeting them at The Hookah Lounge & Bar in East Hartford." Majid in turn traced Aisha's body with the petals.

"Sounds like a plan to me," she acknowledged.

The two of them lay in silence for a while, then Aisha looked up to see a bottle of honey on Majid's nightstand. "Babe, you brought honey into the room? What's it for?" Aisha said, flirting.

"You don't know what it's for? I must have not taught you correctly the first time. Let me show you." Majid pulled Aisha's body underneath his...

Work went by rather slowly for the employees at *Hartford Journal* the next day. Larry gathered everyone into their conference room during the midday for what he called in his corny lingo a "team huddle." He had told the employees one day, "Let's call these meetings team huddles instead. Conference meetings bring stress to my temples. I can feel the ulcers coming."

He always concluded with a geeky chuckle that made Aisha roll her eyes, as it slightly irritated her.

Everyone huddled into the conference room, showing their alliances by sitting with those that they were closest to outside of the job. Larry seemed to observe this as well. He further noticed that Aisha always came to those team huddles by herself and sat next to whoever had an open seat next to them even though she was closest to Kelsey. Larry always saw Aisha as a natural leader. She had her associates on the job but kept her identity; he was intrigued by that.

Larry clapped his hands together. "Well, all righty. Shall we get started?" Larry had an enthusiastic look on his face. His employees just looked back with expressionless stares. "Yeah, well, team, Julia and I had a meeting with the executives, and we've got some startling news to share. As you all know, *Hartford Journal* is ranked third locally in Hartford and tenth in the state of Connecticut. We have not been meeting our goals like we have aspired to. Our goals for the year 2012 were to be first locally and climb to fifth statewide. We have remained like a steady steamboat floating along, not moving down or up, and our bigwig executives believe it is time for some cutbacks. Team, I am fighting this as much as I can. I truly see the talent in all of you, and I have been able to stall these cutbacks at least until the end of this year, after the holidays, of course. I know most of you all have children, and, well, let's just say I don't need my tires slashed.," Larry gave a nervous laugh.

No one responded, so Larry continued. "In the past years, I've noticed our team has gotten very cliquish. Larry sees all. Every time we have a team meeting, you all sit next to your buddies and give dirty looks to your enemies across the table. This is inappropriate behavior, folks. We need a camaraderie team pickup. I want to use everyone's brains in here, preferably Jared's, but, um...everyone's brain in here. We are going to share topics and stories. I will write them on the board, and everyone will leave with a story we all thought of together as a team. That's the plan. I need everyone to open their mouths and speak. I do not want to have to call anyone out." Larry sent a blatant look at Marissa, who was known to be the quiet one on the team, though very smart. She was also the youngest but didn't have the confidence to speak up.

Larry wrote on the dry erase board: "Articles That Will Save Jobs." He double underlined the title and looked at his staff. Jared had an arrogant expression on his face and coughed a bit and remained quiet, keeping his arms crossed. Marissa was the type in the office to write everything in her pad that Larry did, so she wrote down in her notebook the sarcastic title and waited for someone to speak.

Larry looked around the room and stopped at Marissa. He could see the wheels spinning in her head. "Oh, come on. Look, if you all participate, you can add an additional thirty minutes just for this week only to your lunch breaks; do I have your interest now?" Larry asked.

Jared smirked and spoke first. "There is a story one of my sources told me about on the natural food store emporium. Not all of the vitamins and meat they sell is natural, and their fruits and vegetables are not locally grown as they advertise them to be. In fact, a source said they were genetically modified. If someone were to do a story on this, our ranking would definitely pick up locally. Of the West Hartford community, I would say around eighty percent are consumers of the emporium. If I were looking to save my job here, I would start with this story," Jared said, picking the dirt out of his fingernails.

"As always, Jared delivers. Thank you, Jared." Larry continued to write the premise of the story down on the dry erase board. "Folks, I don't want to only hear Marissa's pen vigorously writing. I did not say whose job is at stake, so everyone needs to be writing," Larry said. His staff reluctantly took their pens and began to slowly write. "OK, anyone else?" Larry asked.

Marissa looked around first and shot her hand up after seeing no one was adding anything.

Larry laughed and said, "Marissa, you can just say it out loud."

"How about the old warehouse down on Birch Tree Lane? I heard they hired illegal immigrants to work in that sewing mill and aren't paying them fair wages," Marissa said quietly.

"Why should they pay them fair wages? They're not here legally. Taking all of the American jobs away," Jared shot at Marissa.

Since this was the first time Marissa had ever said anything in the meetings, Larry decided it would be best to not discourage her. "Sounds interesting, Marissa. See what else you can find out. Looks like you just got yourself your article. Good job. Anybody else want to save their job today?" Larry asked derisively.

"Well, I did notice the lake by Willow Street. I have this tradition with my dad where we go finishing down there a couple of times a month, and we detected what looked to be oil in the lake. I wonder if those oil companies are at it again with spilling their oil into the reservoir," Kelsey said, looking concerned about the birds and fish.

"I guess blondes are smart and caring," Jared said, giving Kelsey an approving look after she gave her contribution.

"Oh, how nice of you, Kelsey, to give input even though you're safe," Larry said, writing on the dry erase board.

"Well, just so I know—since you're declaring who is safe—can I think of myself as one of the safe ones? I mean, I am not a blonde, but I've been told I think like one at times," Antoine joked.

Everyone in the room laughed, and the ice was finally broken. The huddle went well, with everyone thinking of a good article to write and with the usually quiet members speaking up during the meeting.

"Good job, team. Well, my conscience is cleared. You all have your articles. Some are better than others on the board here. Of course, thanks to Jared for his great wit. Also, folks, no one in this room is your enemy. Remember that we are a team and should treat each other with respect. This meeting—excuse me—*huddle* is adjourned," Larry said, wiping his hands off from the dry erase markers.

"Great! Now I can go back to hating everyone," Tameka joked. Each one gave an honest laugh at Tameka's remark, knowing that was exactly what everyone was going to do anyway, as well as keep to their cliques.

Aisha walked Kelsey to her cubicle since hers was farther from the conference room. They always reviewed their huddles and talked about people. "Jared is digging you heavy. That was the first time he expressed with words in front of everyone his infatuation for you. That was funny," Aisha said, her eyes opening wide at the thought.

Kelsey grinned and did not say anything.

"Hmm. OK, getting your little office romance on, so I see. Well, I am all for you staying on Jared's good side since it seems to be keeping me employed," Aisha whispered.

Kelsey laughed at the statement. "I'll be your eyes and ears to what is going down, by all means. Jared knows we're cool, but I guess he doesn't care, so he must not hate you," Kelsey said, typing in her password to get back to her work screen on her computer.

"Guess what? Majid wants me to take the assignment," Aisha said, sitting back in Kelsey's visitor's chair.

"He'd better if he wants you to stay employed," Kelsey said, writing up an article on her computer.

"Well, the thing is, he still believes it is a trip to Mumbai for a month and that I'm going to be there with a friend of mine, Chandi." Aisha sent a guilty look toward Kelsey.

"Why didn't you give him the details? Don't you have to provide him flight and hotel information? You're going to have to tell him the truth eventually." Kelsey continued to type.

"I wanted to tell him last night, but let's just say that I would have been an idiot to interrupt the evening we had." Aisha looked up at the ceiling and recalled her romantic night with Majid. "Anyways, we're going to a hookah lounge tonight with some of Majid's friends from Atlanta. I am going to tell him tonight. He will be in a good mood, and we have a rule in our relationship: we never argue in public. So if he is upset, he will do his best to hide it until we get home. Also, if his friends seem to think it is a good career move and express it to him, he will probably agree with them; he's known Mel forever," Aisha explained.

"That sounds like fun. Hookah is a smoker's paradise. Enjoy, doll," Kelsey concluded.

Aisha walked back to her desk to complete an article on a local Nigerian whiz kid who entered high school at the age of twelve. After her article was complete, she sent it to the company's copy editor, shut down her computer, and grabbed her purse. She was one of the last people to leave the office around six o'clock. She placed her khaki trench coat on and hurried to the elevators. She rushed when she saw the elevator closing slowly; she pushed her purse in between the elevator doors.

Larry noticed Aisha and immediately pushed the button to open the elevator.

Oh no! It's Larry. Damn it! Why did I have to rush to the elevator? Aisha thought to herself. She managed a friendly greeting with a smile and stood next to him on the elevator.

"Benson, I trust you are in deep thought about the Kolkata assignment," Larry said sternly, holding his briefcase in front of him.

"Why, yes, sir. I will be providing you an answer soon." Aisha kept close attention to the floor levels they were passing, eager to reach the lobby.

"Well, you've got five more days, Benson. See you tomorrow." Larry motioned his left hand for her to leave the elevator first. "Ladies first," he said.

Aisha gave a shy smile and walked out of the elevator toward the parking garage.

Hookah Pipes & Dinner Play
हुक्का का पाइप एवं रात्रिभोज का मंचन

It was nine o'clock, and Majid parked his Toyota Camry a block down from the Hookah Lounge & Bar in East Hartford. It was a cool October evening, and he had on his leather jacket and a UCONN Huskies fitted hat. He pulled Aisha into him. "I was hoping you'd wear that sexy dress I bought you. But you know what? Those pants show off your body just as much," Majid said into her ear as he chewed his gum.

Aisha had on a winter-white turtleneck tank top shirt, tight black jeans, and Jessica Simpson pumps. She wore a black tie-up sweater over her white shirt.

The two had just made it around the corner, and Majid opened the bar's door for Aisha. "You did something different with your hair?" Majid noticed just as Aisha walked through the door before him.

"Obviously, I flat ironed it, honey." Aisha sent a silly look toward Majid.

He touched her hair, "Ahh, yes. Now I can run my fingers through it. Hmm, that's given me ideas for later tonight," Majid whispered in her ear, standing behind her.

"Behave! Hey, isn't that Mel over there?" Aisha asked, pointing toward Majid's friend who she had seen before in photos.

Mel and Tonya were sitting in a booth. Mel had his arm around Tonya's shoulders, and they both were looking around, bobbing their heads to the music. Majid took Aisha by the hand and brought her over to their table.

"Wassup, dude?" Majid said, hugging his friend.

"We we're just discussing how cold it is up here. We head back to the ATL in a couple of days. So this must be the special lady," Mel said glancing at Aisha.

"Absolutely. Isha, meet Mel and Tonya." Majid introduced everyone.

Aisha hugged Mel and shook Tonya's hand. The group talked for a little in between looking over the various tobacco selections offered.

"What type does your lady like, Mel?" Majid asked his friend.

"Oh, Tonya. She doesn't smoke. She just came for the conversation and atmosphere," Mel said, gazing at his wife.

"I've been trying to get Isha to cut down on smoking. On our second date, I took her to a hookah bar. I remember her: she looked so innocent and timid. She took her first inhale of a hookah pipe, and it was a wrap from there," Majid said, staring at Aisha.

"So not true. I mean, I do smoke, but I don't want to be the only bad girl at the table," Aisha said, nudging her man.

"You all are too cute. Are wedding bells to be expected in the near future? Should Mel and I get another plane ticket ready soon?" Tonya asked.

As Majid was thinking of how to respond, a waitress walked over to the group. "Welcome to the Hookah Lounge & Bar. Which brands of tobacco have you all selected?" the petite brunette asked.

Majid and Mel looked down at the selection. "Let's go with our usual Tangiers Lucid. That's not as heavy as the Shisha," Mel said.

Majid nodded in approval, and the waitress walked away. Aisha looked at Majid, anticipating his answer to Tonya's question.

"We'll keep you all posted on that," Majid said, returning Aisha's stare.

Aisha rolled her eyes, looked at Tonya, and responded in her best imitation of Majid's voice, "We'll keep you posted." The group laughed.

The waitress returned with the tobacco. Majid filled the hookah machine with the tobacco, and Aisha, Mel, and Majid each grabbed a hose.

Majid glanced over at Tonya peeking at them. "Are you sure you don't wanna partake? You only live once, you know, and if we do incarnate, I might as well get my hands somewhat dirty to remind me of the experience I had before," Majid jokingly pressured.

"No thanks. Not for me. I'm not a goody-two-shoes or anything, but it's just not for me," Tonya said, looking at her husband.

"She's lying. She is a goody-two-shoes, but that's why I married her. I figured angels were becoming a dying breed in our world." Mel took his wife's hand and kissed it.

"Aww," Majid and Aisha said in harmony. They looked at each other intently in the eyes and sucked on the hookah pipe in unison. Once they inhaled enough smoke, they held it in their mouths and kissed passionately, allowing the smoke to blow from their lips and up to the ceiling.

Mel stopped sucking on the hookah pipe to watch the show Majid and Aisha were putting on. "Hmph. It must be good. Remember when we were like that?" Mel asked his wife.

After hearing Mel's comment, Tonya shot her husband a displeased look. "After being pregnant with your first child, I can't seem to remember anything. But, no, I don't think it was ever that intense for us, especially not in public," Tonya said, feeling like she was watching a moment that should have been private between Majid and Aisha.

"Right, we never were like that because you think Jesus would have a problem," Mel teased his wife.

"Hmph. I guess they don't believe in coming up for air," Tonya said blatantly in their direction.

Majid removed his hand from Aisha's hair and licked his lips as he slowly parted from Aisha's mouth. He whispered in her ear, "I love the bad girl in you." Turning back to his friend, Majid asked, "So, tell us: How is the baby girl?"

"Briana is such a sweet little girl. She hardly gives us problems. She is with her grandparents now. We usually have a date night at least once a month, so we had to leave the little joy with Mel's parents," Tonya said, showing them a picture of their daughter.

"You know, babe, Tonya has written like four books. She is a self-published author," Majid said, trying to find a commonality between Aisha and Tonya. "My lady here works at *Hartford Journal* as a journalist," Majid announced.

"Oh, really? I see you and my wife have writing in common, Aisha. So man how is UCONN these days?"

Mel and Majid discussed work, and Aisha walked around the booth to sit next to Tonya.

"It's hard to hear you with the music blasting," Aisha said, plopping down next to Tonya.

"Oh, yeah, definitely. That and I also tend to have a soft speaking voice. I found my more expressive voice in writing," Tonya said, smiling.

"I hear you. So are you an Atlanta native?" Aisha asked.

"Yes, I am. There are so few nowadays that live there. Most of my close girlfriends are from the northeast—well, except two of them. They are ATL born and raised like me. In fact, I just went out with them last week. I have a girlfriend, bless her heart, who is being sued by her boss. It's a big scandal in Atlanta, all over the ATL news. I bet if you worked as a columnist down there you'd want this story," Tonya said.

"Really? So how far into the trial are you all?" Aisha asked.

"It's been five months since June. It's that boyfriend of hers; he is caught up in some criminal scheme. I know love when I see it, and honestly I've never seen my girl Sabrina so in love or seen two people who looked to be so right for one another. But I do not know about them being able to survive this. If I was on trial because of my man's actions, I doubt I'd stay with him," Tonya said.

"Hmm, she must be crazy in love. So how does he look?" Aisha whispered so that the fellas did not hear them.

"Like God took his time creating a masterpiece," Tonya whispered back.

"Your girl must be a looker herself?" Aisha chatted back.

Tonya thought about it. "Sabrina is pretty. She could go for a slimmer version of the actress Keisha Pulliam. She's got that girl-next-door look, minus the pretty hair. My girl wears hair extensions." Aisha and Tonya laughed. "In fact, her mother told mine that when she was younger, whenever Sabrina went out, until she was like seven years old, people at times would stop them anywhere—on the streets, the grocery store, etc.—to ask Sabrina's mom if she was Keisha Pulliam or a relative of hers; true story. She looked very similar to her when she was younger."

Tonya continued, "We always tease Bri about her good girl image because it is so not necessary now. We are in our thirties, but I guess that's a part of my girl's charm; it won Tyrone's heart," Tonya said, chewing her gum.

"Her good-looking, trouble-making boyfriend's name is Tyrone. I never liked that name," Aisha expressed, shaking her head.

"Apparently, he never cared for it either, so he goes by Ty," Tonya added. "I could tell when Bri got serious with him because she never gave us dirt on him. I was proud of her. We have this other girlfriend who is a serial dater of mostly athletes, and she has always tried to get a story out of Bri; I'm glad she never gave her any details. My girlfriends know not to ask me since they call me *choir girl*," Tonya jokingly said.

"Yeah, you do seem a bit uptight," Aisha said, laughing.

"You wanna see a pic of my crew?" Tonya took out her phone and showed a photo of her and her girlfriends taken at a nightclub.

"Cute! You girls look like a multiethnic *Sex and the City*," Aisha said, returning Tonya her phone.

"Yep, that's my crew—love them to death." Tonya placed her phone back into her purse.

"Listen, why don't we exchange numbers? I would love to hear how your friend fares with this trial," Aisha said, taking her phone out. Aisha text messaged her phone number along with e-mail address to Tonya.

"I'll keep you abreast. I pray for my girl every day. Would hate to have to visit Bri in prison though; orange is so not her color." Aisha and Tonya laughed.

Aisha put down the hookah pipe and placed her head back on the booth with the upholstered cushions. "I feel lightheaded—almost like a contact high," Aisha said, brushing her hair back and crossing her legs.

Majid looked at Aisha as he walked over to the side of the booth she sat in. "Just relax, babe. You probably inhaled too much. Tangiers Lucid is the less heavy one too; my lady is a lightweight," Majid said, touching her forehead just to make sure she was not developing a fever.

"I'm good, honey. Just gonna chill on that. You and Mel enjoy," Aisha said.

Majid exhaled out of the hookah pipe and said, "My lady just got asked to be on assignment in Mumbai."

"Awesome. So when do you leave?" Mel asked Aisha.

Aisha had nervously anticipated the conversation coming around to her assignment, so she gave a tense smile and said, "Well, the assignment is approaching in a couple of weeks, actually. Mumbai was a rumor; the assignment is really in Kolkata." Aisha fiddled with her phone in her hand, waiting for Majid's reaction. He did a double take.

"Kolkata—interesting. I have never been to India before, so I cannot relate. But it sounds like an adventure awaits you," Mel said, observing Majid's facial expression.

Majid, remembering the rule of their relationship, *Never argue in public*, laughed off this new information and inhaled the tobacco smoke. Mel noticed the change in his friend's behavior and just remained quiet for a minute or two, enjoying the hookah pipe. Majid broke the silence after a while, asking, "Mel, how would you feel if Tonya had to go on a book signing tour for a month or so and one of the destinations was out of the country?"

"I would be concerned. That's my lady. But it's also her career, and I don't want to slow her down," Mel said, looking at Majid sternly. "By the way, she has gone on book tours; she had a book signing in London a year ago," Mel said, speaking for his wife. "That time away, which was like two months, was sort of refreshing because I got to miss her. When she came back, well, you know the rest of the story: Briana was conceived." Mel kissed his wife on the cheek. "Hey, Aisha, if I were you, I'd go. I guarantee when you get back, my dude will propose because he will realize what he's been missing." Mel winked at Aisha.

"Hmm, good point. Did not think of that," Aisha said, staring at her man. Mel laughed at Majid.

"Tell'n all the secrets, I see. Thought we were boys," Majid sarcastically stated.

Majid was silent in the car all the way back to West Hartford. Aisha knew she was in for it when they arrived home.

As she undressed in their bedroom, she broke the silence. "Babe, I need you to talk to me. I really need your support on this. Please be honest with me. Are you OK with this?" She placed on her robe and lay on the bed.

Majid undressed down to his boxers and tank top. "I don't know how I feel, Isha. I was coming around to the idea of a Mumbai relocation. Kolkata is another story. That's in West Bengal, and you would be in India for real. My American girl in one of the realest states of India—you stress'n me, woman." Majid got on the bed with Aisha.

"I have to provide an answer to Larry Monday. There is more to the story. Apparently the *Hartford Journal* is doing cutbacks. My name was on the chopping block, love. Larry explained to me that if I get my hands on a particular story, I could impress the corporate executives, depending on how I cleverly write it. As a result, my job will be saved." Aisha cradled her knees to her chest.

"This was all told to you, really?" Majid asked.

"Yes. In fact, we had a team huddle today, and Larry announced cutbacks to be expected at the end of the year. In order for me to keep this job, I need to take this story and deliver on it," she said.

Majid breathed in and exhaled slowly. "Well, you have been working for the company for five years, right?" Aisha nodded. "You're thirty years old now. You're not someone fresh out of college. You've made your name at the *Hartford Journal*, so it makes sense for you to remain there. To start somewhere else at your age, you'd have to start all over again, and technically, you're just beginning to grow where you are," Majid said, thinking out loud.

Aisha smiled. She knew in the years of being with him that if he thought out loud about something, he was heavily considering it. "Yes and...?" Aisha wanted him to continue.

Majid looked at her sternly. "Tomorrow I am going to send an attachment to your work e-mail. Forward the e-mail to your boss. It will be a list of questions about this trip, and I know some of these questions you would not think to ask him. So was the duration of time on assignment a rumor too?" he asked.

Aisha nodded. "The assignment is actually for three months," she said quietly.

"Hmph. I am going to get ready for bed. We've talked about this enough. I will send the e-mail to you tomorrow afternoon." Majid kissed Aisha on the forehead and headed into the bathroom to take a shower.

Aisha rolled over onto her stomach and thought about their conversation. "That conversation did not go as bad as I thought," she said and waited her turn to get in the shower.

It was Friday afternoon, and Aisha and Kelsey got back from their hour-and-a-half lunch break. Aisha went back to her cubicle and typed her password in to be logged back into her work screen. She checked her e-mails and noticed Majid had sent her the e-mail about the relocation. Before she forwarded the attachment, she read what he wrote:

> Isha,
> Make sure you send Larry these questions for your relocation. I know you are pretty certain the assignment would only be three months, but you need everything in writing. See you at home.
> —Majid

Aisha smirked at his concern and looked over the questions he provided:

1) Will job relocation guarantee advancement in my career?
2) Does this job relocation coincide with a promotion? Should I expect a pay increase?
3) What are the consequences if I do not relocate?
4) Will the *Hartford Journal* pay for my work visa?
5) How long is the relocation for the assignment supposed to last?
6) How will *Hartford Journal* help me to assimilate into this new country as an expatriate?
7) How will *Hartford Journal* help me to assimilate back to the United States as a repatriate?

"Not bad, babe," Aisha said after reading. She composed a new e-mail for Larry and attached Majid's questions.

As Aisha worked on another story, Marissa walked into her cubicle. "Wassup, Ish?" Marissa said and sat in the visitor's chair.

"Hey, Marissa. How is your new story going?" Aisha said, engaging her.

"Not so bad. It's sort of off to a slow start. I have someone peeking around the old sewing mill, and it looks like they hired a bunch of workers, but they cannot confirm for me if they are here illegally yet." Marissa picked up the Rubik's Cube.

Everyone loves that thing, Aisha thought, seeing Marissa fuss with it. "I'm glad you are not letting Jared discourage you. He thinks he's all that, and Larry encourages that type of behavior from him only," Aisha said.

"I know. I noticed how he seems to always control the meetings—oops!—I mean huddles. Larry really does not control them, which looks bad on him," Marissa said. "Well, you know corporate politics. Jared is the one with the best stories. He does keep our paper in the ranks we are in, so I can't hate on him," she further said.

"Well, he also gets more encouragement from Larry than the rest of us. Antoine, Chris Santos, or Jamal could have a great idea, and he will just write it down on the dry erase board and not praise them for their topic. But the minute Jared thinks of a story—even just an OK story—it's all of a sudden the best topic he has ever heard. It's like he's grooming Jared for a higher position and letting the rest of us know he is the best. I don't think that's fair," Aisha said.

"Well, you know why." Marissa pointed to her skin complexion.

"Absolutely," Aisha agreed.

"I see sometimes how the brothas on the team act with Larry. They look at him like they want to rip his head off, and I don't blame them. He will never acknowledge their talent; he just overlooks them constantly. You noticed how anytime Chris, Jamal, or Antoine was about to speak in our huddle, Larry would interrupt them until they looked aggravated, and then he would smile and say, 'OK, continue.' It's like a game with him. But when a sista speaks, he will listen to what we have to say and never interrupt us," Marissa said.

"Because he's not intimated by a female. That's why," Aisha added.

The women talked for a while about the office politics until Marissa saw Larry walking down the hallway.

"Gotta go. Here comes unibrow. TTYL!" Marissa rushed into her cubicle, which was diagonal from Aisha's.

"Benson, those were some interesting questions," Larry said as he got to Aisha's cubicle.

"Well, sir, you did say I can ask anything between now and Monday," she said.

"Right, but Monday it's either yes or no, and it would be in your best interest to say yes." Larry nodded at her. "In any event, they've been answered, so please check your e-mail. See you Monday with a response back," Larry said. "I am leaving for the day. You know Fridays tend to be half days for me. I get to play golf." He smiled and walked toward the elevator.

Aisha rolled her eyes and reviewed his answers:

1) Will job relocation guarantee advancement in my career?

It's a strong possibility, depending upon the interest it draws from our readers.

2) Does this job relocation coincide with a promotion? Should I expect a pay increase?

Again, strong possibility, depending upon the interest it draws from our readers.

3). What are the consequences if I do not relocate?

I believe you know the answer to this...

4) Will the *Hartford Journal* pay for my work visa?

Absolutely. We will provide you with a corporate card to place all living expenses on, as well as food, hotel, and transportation.

5) How long is the relocation for the assignment supposed to last?

As we discussed in the office: three months, leaving the third week in October and coming back the third week in December; just in time for Saint Nicholas ☺.

6) How will *Hartford Journal* help me to assimilate into this new country as an expatriate?

Lydia developed a solid rapport with someone from the US Consulate of Kolkata, Nivritti Yadav. She is from West Bengal but went to college in the United States; she embodies the ideal blend of West and East culture. She volunteered to be your liaison between the United States and Kolkata. She will be your interpreter/translator, as some of the women in the brothels do not speak English. She can also be your guide, give you a tour of Kolkata, and show you around to the food markets, shopping malls, and the safer areas to get transportation. Also during your time at the brothels, we will have the US Consulate guarding you. You will not meet these people, but they will know who you are during your stay and will be protecting you from an arm's length.

7) How will *Hartford Journal* help me to assimilate back to the United States as a repatriate?

You think you'll be gone so long you will not remember what being an American is? LOL. Benson, you will have two days when you get back to readjust to the time zone, but we are going to need you e-mail us your story before you leave India, as well as additional photos or other items you can think of. Leave all documents with the consulate; they will send them back to the States.

Remember: MONDAY I need an answer. Happy Friday!

"OK, well, Majid should relax. I got his questions answered. Who cares about Christmas anyway? He forgot I am Muslim," Aisha said out loud, responding to Larry's answer for her fifth question. She printed out the e-mail and placed it in her purse.

☾

Aisha got home later than Majid, who was in the kitchen, fixing dinner. "Hey, lovey," Aisha said and kissed his lips.

"Has your boss gotten back to you about those questions I sent you?" Majid asked, grabbing red and yellow peppers out of the refrigerator and placing them on the cutting board.

"Yes, he did. Would you like for me to leave the printout on your nightstand?" she said, showing him the paper.

"Please," Majid responded, cutting the peppers.

Aisha went into their bedroom, undressed down to her undergarments, put on pink yoga pants and a white sports bra, and returned to the kitchen.

"Haven't seen you wear that in a while," Majid said, looking her up and down.

"I know. I didn't realize how many clothes I have," she said, glimpsing around to see how she could help Majid.

Majid noticed her glancing around. "You want to help? You can cut that onion over there, and then in that bowl place in a quarter teaspoon of turmeric powder. See the poppy seeds that are over in that bowl, soaking in water? Place four tablespoons of those into that mixing bowl, cut two cloves of garlic into the bowl, and add a quarter teaspoon of black mustard seeds," Majid said to her.

"Boy, please! How am I supposed to remember all of that?" Aisha said, cutting the onion.

Majid walked over to her with the recipe and looked her up and down. He went behind her and nudged her with his manhood. "Here you go," he said, moving her hair out of the way to kiss her neck. He looked down at her sports bra and playfully fondled her chest. "Must be cold in here, huh?" A smile formed on Majid's face, and he walked back over to their kitchen's island.

Aisha rolled her eyes, peeked down, and noticed what made him say that. "Whatever. This must be a new dish: Posto Rang Bahar. Did I pronounce it correctly?" she asked.

"No, but you can pronounce it however you want in that outfit," Majid said, getting the mustard oil out of their pantry. "You know, it's my brother's birthday tomorrow, and I thought we'd make a big pot of this and take some over to my parents' home tomorrow evening. Sunday we can just kick it. I have to put together a midterm review for my students," he said.

"Eww, you just gave me a flashback to college; midterms already?" Aisha asked.

"Yep, it's a dirty job, but someone's gotta do it. My students love me though. They told me today I was one of the coolest professors on campus." Majid smirked.

"Who did? The girls or the guys?" Aisha asked.

Majid thought about her question. "It was mostly females, but some of my male students agreed."

"Oh, please. Those girls just like the way you look. If I were still in college, I would enroll in your Biochemistry course too and would look forward to afterschool tutoring as well." Aisha turned around and looked at Majid.

"If you were my student, somebody would be in trouble," Majid flirted back but kept a serious tone of voice.

"I think we need to role play student/teacher tonight." Aisha walked over to Majid and put in front of his mouth a spoonful of turmeric powder, panch phoron—which is a mixture of five spices—the poppy seeds that had emulsified into the mix, and garlic with the chili sauce on it. She placed some of the mixture on her nose. Majid took his tongue and lightly licked the sauce off her nose and kissed down to her mouth.

He pointed for her to insert the spoon in is his mouth. "Mmm... luscious. The sauce isn't bad either. Needs some salt though," Majid said, pointing for Aisha to place the salt into the mix. The two cooked and romantically played with one another until the dish was complete.

"Babe, can you pass me the rice?" Majid asked as they sat at their dining room table, enjoying the meal.

"So how old is Naji going to be?" Aisha asked.

Majid never cared for conversing during his meal because he always thought it was rude to chew food while speaking to someone. He waited to answer the question until his food went down his throat. "He is twenty-six now and should be moved out of our parents' home," Majid added. "When I was twenty-two, I graduated from college, left home, and never came back. That boy is spoiled."

"Well, he is the baby," Aisha responded. "Maybe he's waiting to get married first before he leaves the nest."

"No woman wants to marry a man who lives with his parents. But my mom still does his laundry and cooks for him. She's making life real comfortable for him to remain home. If he can't find a woman soon to marry, it's her fault," Majid said, holding his fork before placing the food in his mouth. "I have a feeling they will pick a friend of the family's for him anyway," he concluded.

"You did tell me they treat you like the black sheep of the family," Aisha said.

Majid nodded. "Basically, but it does not bother me anymore. I don't depend on my parents for anything, and they've gotten used to us together. Would they rather you were Bengali? Probably so, but they know I love you, and they have grown to love you as well." Majid placed the food in his mouth. When he was through swallowing, he continued, "I have done everything my parents wanted me to do. My mom brags to family all the time that I went to college, graduated summa cum laude, that I am a biochemistry professor; they cannot ask for anything more. I remember coming home from school and, I kid you not, Isha, if I ever received a grade lower than a B, I got punished," Majid said. "Most of my grades were As and Bs; I did get one C in English in elementary school, and my mom was so disappointed in me that for a whole week she did not allow me to play with my friends outside. And I had to ditch basketball practice that entire week and come home to study right after school. But in college I got nothing less than a B. So, in saying all of that, I've become the man they wanted me to be. Who I choose to have in my bed with me at night is neither under their control nor their business," Majid finished.

"Well, that's probably why she never gave her opinion of me to you when we first started dating but waited until she noticed we got serious," Aisha said.

Majid nodded and cleaned his mouth with his napkin. "A'ight, baby girl, I am going to chill for a bit in the bedroom and read this e-mail Larry answered you back with." Majid got up from the table and went into their room. Aisha finished her food and cleaned up the kitchen.

☾

Majid was in their bed, with his boxers on and no shirt. He had on his reading glasses and was looking down at the e-mail. "Your boss is condescending," he said.

"Oh, you took notice of his little comments as well, huh? He told me if I had any questions that I shouldn't hesitate to ask. I hate when people say something but don't really mean it." She got under the covers next to him in bed.

He continued to ponder the e-mail.

"Professor Khan, I'm sure you've read over this e-mail a million times. There are only seven questions listed. So, are we ready to play?" Aisha slowly pulled the paper away from Majid and placed it on her nightstand. She began to suck his fingers. Majid slowly removed his glasses with his free hand. "Keep the glasses on. It adds to the fantasy," Aisha said in between sucking his fingers.

"Well, Ms. Benson, what do you want me to teach you tonight?" Majid put his reading glasses back on.

"I'm such an avid learner, as you know, so I hope you have the stamina to teach me everything" She removed her robe and got on top of him...

Being a Khan
खान होने के कारण

"Majid and Aisha, come in," Majid's mom said, greeting the couple at the door.

The couple had arrived at the Khan residence Saturday evening for the celebration of Naji's birthday. Majid hugged his mother and helped Aisha step out of her ballet flats and place them inside of a cupboard near the doorway. He took his shoes off as well and walked with her into the home. The Khan residence was located in Middletown, around thirty minutes from Majid and Aisha's condo. His parents lived in an old Victorian house with five bedrooms and three and a half baths, one being a powder room downstairs for guests. The house was a block from the Connecticut River and Harbor Park.

Aisha wore a traditional black *khimar* with a maroon-colored trimming design sewn around it. She was used to the attire since as a young woman she had dressed this way until she went to college. She took a course in college called The Discovery of Mystery, which went into detail analyzing Eastern and Western religions. It was her favorite course and changed her way of looking at things.

She began to have an appreciation for practices, customs, and rituals of all religions, but having grown up in a Muslim household, she felt almost an internal struggle to keep with the tradition she was born into. A year into their relationship, Majid described to Aisha that he wanted her to meet his family. He explained that like her he grew up in a Muslim household. When there was a celebration for something in his family, he always wanted her to show respect at the Khan residence by wearing formal Muslim attire.

Aisha walked into the family room to see Majid's younger cousins playing board games. His aunts and uncles were across the hallway in the living room, watching the news. As Majid and Aisha passed into the family room, they greeted everyone, and Aisha looked intently at a novel on the coffee table, almost hypnotized by the beauty of the Hindi script.

Majid noticed her stare. "Oh, my family's favorite Bengali author." He picked the book up. "Mir Mosharraf Hossain; this is the book on his life. You know, we have some of his work in our condo. You should read one of his most famous plays called *Jamidar Darpan*." He placed the book back down in the center of the table.

"*The Landlord Exposed*: it spoke of the plight of the average, common person in Bangladesh under the strict rule of the zamindars, those who were set up by the British colonial rulers to control the people, and it illustrates the struggles our people faced," Mrs. Khan finished. "My dear, you look lovely." Mrs. Khan approved of Aisha's attire and took from her the Posto Rang Bahar dish she and Majid had fixed.

Aisha accompanied Mrs. Khan into the kitchen to help set the table for everyone, and Majid walked up the stairs to his brother's room. There were photos hung along the railing of their home that brought humble memories back to him of his younger years.

He knocked on his brother's door. "Wassup, li'l bro? Happy birthday, man." Majid handed him his present.

"Hmm, doesn't look like money. Let's see." Naji placed the gift down.

"Like you need money. Please," Majid said.

"I'll be formal, brother, and wait until you leave to open the gift," Naji said, placing it on his bed.

"Open it now. Come on. No one is watching. Mom and Dad are downstairs," Majid urged.

"All right, man." Naji tore through the wrapping paper and read the cover of the novel. "*Samaresh Basu's Short Stories*—good choice, even though he is Hindi," Naji joked.

The two walked downstairs, and as they came into the dining room, they looked around the table. "Mom went all out as usual," Majid said. The table was adorned with traditional Bengali decorations for family celebrations and traditional foods. The Khans' wedding china was also out. The women came into the room and placed on everyone's plate a bowl of thin soup known as *dal*.

Majid looked at Aisha and noticed how comfortable and domesticated she looked around his family, and he loved the fact that she wanted to help his mother. The look he gave her was one that seemed to make time itself stop. She gave a flirtatious look with her eyes and smiled as she went back into the kitchen to get more food.

Naji noticed the moment between his brother and Aisha. "So, does Mom need to prepare some *biryani* soon?" Naji looked over at his brother.

"I'll keep you posted on that, but enough about my business. Are you dating anyone now?" Majid responded.

"Here and there. I was seeing a girl from Oklahoma, but she moved back there since she could not find any work after she graduated from Wesleyan."

"Boys, get the family. It's time to sit down at the table," Mrs. Khan said from the kitchen.

The Khan family took their seats to enjoy their meal and conversation at the dinner table. Mr. Khan sat at the head of the table and, like Majid, preferred to be silent until he was finished eating. When he was done with the first course, he patted his mouth with his napkin and decided to get involved in conversation. Every time a family member spoke in English, Mr. Khan would add something in their native Bengali language. After a while everyone followed Mr. Khan's behavior and began speaking in their native dialect.

This made Majid very uncomfortable. He had asked many years ago, once he got serious with Aisha, that whenever an American friend came to the house for everyone to speak in English out of respect to the guest. Because Majid and Naji respected their father as the man of the house, they never corrected him in front of family. Mr. Khan continued to speak in their native language, and Majid coughed uncomfortably. Mrs. Khan noticed her son's behavior for what it was and told her husband through their native language to speak in English. Once she said that, everyone smiled in Aisha's direction, and she smiled back in a confused manner. She shrugged her shoulders to Majid when she noticed the conversation had stopped and his family stared at her.

Majid put his arm around her chair, looked at his family defiantly, and started a new conversation. "So, Dad, at UCONN they have a growing Indian student population. The Indian students just organized an Indian Student Association and are celebrating *Diwali* next week."

Mr. Khan nodded his head. "Well, that's good, son. It is a Hindu celebration, and Bengalis usually do not celebrate this, but are you their academic advisor?"

Majid smiled. "Yes, I am one of the two Indian professors who are tenured and well respected by the rest of the faculty on campus there. So when the students approached me, I felt it was my duty to provide my support."

Aisha smiled, proud of her man.

"Well, son, out of those Indian students in the association, how many are Bengali?" Mr. Khan asked.

"I did not ask. Many do not know I am Muslim. I prefer to not bring up religious beliefs at work since I work around a mostly Christian faculty. You know, speaking of careers, Aisha has been asked to relocate for a couple of months on a journalism assignment," Majid said, changing the subject.

The Khan family nodded in approval and looked at Aisha to finally contribute to the family conversation.

Aisha beamed and spoke up. "Yes, my boss asked me if I would be interested in relocating to Kolkata for three months."

Mrs. Khan smiled and nodded. "Why Kolkata? I find that fascinating. Very close to Bangladesh. You should have asked him to go there instead. You could have stayed with one of my relatives."

"Well, Mrs. Khan, there is a story in particular that I am in search of in Kolkata only." Aisha thought about the context of the story and definitely knew it was not the right time to bring up the red-light district. "Apparently, an American journalist decided to move her life to Kolkata, and I am to find this woman and bring back her story. This mysterious woman has lived in Kolkata now for twenty years, and she became a much respected woman by a certain group of people there," Aisha concluded, leaving out the details.

The Khan family was very intrigued by Aisha's conversation. "Will you have an interpreter, dear? South Asians are some of the most traditional Indian people you could ever meet, and a good amount do not speak English," one of Majid's aunts added.

"Yes, I will. She works for the consulate in Kolkata. From what I was told about her, she speaks many languages and went to college in the US," Aisha responded.

"Our family has been to Kolkata. Be careful on the streets, and wear conservative clothing, dear. Do not blatantly be American and wear jeans and short skirts. The men think very differently, and the rules are different there too," Mr. Khan interjected. "I look at American women sometimes on the streets and can't believe that their husbands allow them to go outside with nothing on, and they wonder why men catcall them," he added.

"Well, America is different, honey. When you live in different places in the world, you have to assimilate according to those people's standards. We all do. As a traditional woman myself, I will wear jeans from time to time, but I will wear a sari shirt over them," Mrs. Khan added. "Honey, I hope when you are out with our Majid you dress demurely; he prefers a woman like that." Mrs. Khan looked at her son.

Majid looked up, surprised, but he smiled at his mother and nodded. He quickly shot Aisha a rebellious grin and rubbed her thighs underneath the dining room table.

Aisha thought to herself: *No, he doesn't. He begs me to wear tight clothes when we go out.* But she smiled and nodded at Mrs. Khan's remark. "Of course, Mrs. Khan."

"Well, enjoy, dear. You will see a more traditional side in South Asia and come back Bengali," Mrs. Khan teased and folded her hands on top of the table. "OK, time for the next course."

The women went into the kitchen to help Mrs. Khan carry out more food. There were bowls of vegetables and beef curry brought out, and the women served the men and elderly at the table, spooning the food into their rice bowls. Conversation continued in English, with the younger generations providing entertaining dialogue concerning school and new toys out on the market. The very last course the women served was *doi*, a yogurt dessert dish, which they spooned into the last of each person's rice bowl. After dinner, everyone congregated in the family room, where one of Majid's aunts turned on Bengali music.

Majid helped his paternal grandparents sit in the living room and placed the Dhallywood film *Sadanander Mela* into the DVD player for them to watch. Majid walked back into the family room to hang out with his younger cousins and observed them playfully dance to the rhythmic beats of Bengali music. He noticed Aisha walking down the hallway toward him after assisting his mother clean up the kitchen. She plopped down on a lounge chair in the family room beside Majid.

He kissed her on the cheek and rubbed her temples. "This is what being a Khan is like. Imagine preparing three-course meals for ten people at least once a month," he flirtingly whispered in her ear as he put her feet on his lap and gently rubbed them.

The children in the room stopped dancing and giggled at Majid and Aisha's intimate moment. "Ooh, Majid, you like her," Majid's baby cousin said.

Aisha laughed and placed her feet back on the carpet. Majid picked up his younger male cousin by the collar and said, "Yes, I do. Hopefully when you reach my age you will find someone just like Aisha as well." Majid placed him back down on the carpet. His baby cousin shook his head violently, fixed his shirt, and continued to playfully dance and sing along with the Bengali music.

Majid and Aisha stayed for a while longer sitting in the living room for another hour to watch the Dhallywood film with Majid's grandparents, aunts, and uncles. They wished Naji happy birthday and kissed his parents before heading back home.

Shadow Reign or Aisha Benson?
छद्मनाम या आइसा बेंसन?

At ten o'clock on Monday morning, Aisha knocked confidently on Larry's office door. She heard Larry through the door, speaking to Jared.

"Who is it?" Larry asked.

"It's Aisha, sir." She heard Jared's voice, but his comment was so low she could not make out what he said. Then Larry and Jared both laughed hysterically for a moment or two.

"Come on in, Benson!" Larry finally shouted from behind the door.

Aisha opened his office door. Jared looked up with his eyebrows arched, sitting back comfortably in Larry's visitor's chair. Whatever comment had been made, Aisha could tell that it was about her by noticing their abrupt change in behavior the minute she walked in the office.

She ignored Jared's haughty stare and focused her remarks at Larry. "I thought about the relocation and..." She changed her glance to Jared, waiting for him to get the hint and leave the office.

Larry sensed her feelings and said to Jared, "We'll discuss later, Jared. Hey, man, I love that shirt; you have such impeccable taste."

Jared popped his collar, laughed in Aisha's direction, and walked out of the office.

Aisha rolled her eyes at the brownnosing Larry was doing for Jared and turned back to Larry to finish her thought. "I thought about the relocation, and after careful consideration and speaking with my loved ones and having you answer my questions, I must say...Sign me up. I'm ready for this assignment." Aisha clasped her hands together with an enthusiastic smile.

"Good deal. I was expecting you to say that. Julia and I took the liberty of getting things moving just in case you did say yes, so I have some information to give to you." Larry went inside of his desk and took out a thick binder that had the description: *Hartford Journal* Relocation Assignment Handbook. "Please read over everything in this binder."

Aisha took the binder from Larry and opened to the first flap. It had her work visa and corporate credit card. She took those out and placed them in her pockets.

"Make sure you guard those as if they were your passport or license," Larry said.

Aisha nodded to Larry and turned through the binder. The first page had written on it: West Bengal—Everything the Traveling Journalist Should Know. She saw index tabs labeled with the titles: language, food, festivals, religions, and daily customs. There was also a small glossary in the back that translated common words and phrases from Hindi script to English translation.

"Even though West Bengal is predominantly Muslim, most people acknowledge the shared language as Hindi. This can help you some, but don't worry: we have your interpreter, Nivritti Yadav, who will be accompanying you during your time there," Larry said, noticing Aisha glancing through the binder. "Don't feel overwhelmed, Benson. You asked some great questions and, believe it or not, the last two were really smart questions to ask. We composed this binder to help you assimilate into this new world because it will be a culture shock for you—especially the red-light district. Speaking of which, we have a section for you in here toward the middle of the binder describing it in detail."

Larry got up and assisted Aisha with turning to the tab on the red-light district. Aisha looked over the photographs. There were beautiful Indian women dressed in bare midriff tops and long skirts. They also had henna tattoos adorning their hands and arms and red makeup creating a circular shape in between their thick, black, arched eyebrows. Some also had the red makeup in between a huge middle part in their hair.

"Several of these women look very young," Aisha said, noticing women who looked like they were teenagers.

"The terrible truth is that some are. I told you children can be born into this," Larry said, turning the page.

Aisha looked to another page that described the midriff top as *choli* in West Bengal. "Well, this trip is definitely going to be filled with life lessons for me," Aisha said, feeling slightly overwhelmed by the breadth of information inside of the binder.

"Yes, it is. Nivritti can show you safe marketplaces and tell you how to conduct yourself in town. We also took some information from the US Consulate of Kolkata. Ugh...Turn a couple of tabs through to see this." Larry moved the tabs along to one of the thickest sections of the binder. "This whole tab has facts taken from women who have traveled through South Asia and shared their experience with the consulate. In the last section of this tab are emergency contact numbers; place those into your cell phone as soon as possible," Larry explained to her.

Aisha heard him but was focused on reading a section called Safety for Female Foreign Travelers.

Larry noticed her stare and watched her hand as she pointed to what she read. He said, "Pack mostly traditional South Asian clothing, Benson, for your own safety. There is a phrase that the people there have for umm...women of African descent: *eve teasing*. Women of African descent have reported verbal comments being lashed out at them in public places like markets and train stations..." Larry trailed off.

"Eve teasing? Are you kidding me? It says outright groping! If one of those men even tries to touch me, he's getting slapped in the face," Aisha said.

Larry laughed. "Funny, Benson, you will not be in America, though; you will be in West Bengal, and the rules there are very different. Do not give any of those men a reason to touch you in public. I know here women can wear whatever they want, but there if you're in American short-shorts, it's kind of seen as your fault if a man reacts to you. I know I don't agree with that, and I am all for women's rights, but again, you won't be in Kansas anymore, Benson. Just be mindful of that," Larry said.

Aisha's eyes widened at the cultural difference described in the binder. Larry continued further, "You know, *eve teasing* refers to *Eve* as the original woman. Larry cleared his throat. "Apparently *Eves* are secretly desired women in this part of the world. At least that's what we believe this woman's story to be somewhat about." Larry showed the photo of the mysterious woman again to Aisha.

Aisha looked at the photo. "Got it, sir. She kind of gives me the creeps. I feel like I am staring at an adult picture of me circa the 1990s or something—eerie part being I was a child back then. You can take the photo back now, thanks," Aisha said, her gaze returning to the binder.

Larry smiled and placed the photo back in his desk drawer. "Your flight is scheduled for next Thursday. The total time en route is twenty hours; there is a short layover for you in Frankfurt, Germany—nothing overnight, very short, like an hour wait period. Nivritti will meet you at Netaji Subhas Chandra Bose International Airport in Kolkata once you land Friday. Your tickets are in the last flap of the binder."

Aisha looked toward the back of the binder and pulled out her trip itinerary. "Fantastic. Does she have my cell phone number and photo so she knows what I look like?" Aisha asked, placing the itinerary back into the flap.

"We gave her your cell phone number. And don't worry: she knows what you look like. That woman was known in the red-light district, so we imagine some of the older women there are going to stare when they meet you; it will be like they've seen a ghost, perhaps." Larry chuckled. Aisha looked uncomfortable; Larry stopped chuckling.

"OK. I see I have a lot to digest. Anything else I should know? Like, what is this woman's name?" Aisha got up from the chair and walked toward the door.

"Her American name was Cyndi Jenkins, but the native people do not know her as that," Larry said.

Aisha turned back around before opening his office door. "Well, what do they know her as?" she asked Larry.

"She is known in the red-light district as Black Gold," Larry said uncomfortably.

"Black Gold? Why?" Aisha asked.

"Well, that's for you to find out, Benson, but we can only imagine, being that Lydia found her photo in the red-light district... Need I say more?" Larry awkwardly asked, fidgeting in his office chair.

"Gotcha. Well, I am not that dense, so no need to describe further; I got it." Aisha said.

"Also, Benson, Nivritti made a great suggestion to us for you to remain safe. Once you pass customs, you should introduce yourself to the native people there by your pen name—Shadow Reign—to keep you safe. If the consulate needs to get in touch with you, that is what they will call you, and so will Nivritti the minute you get off the plane. Remember that: in Kolkata your name is Shadow Reign," Larry said very slowly and clearly with a serious expression.

Aisha nodded her head and left Larry's office.

The World's Oldest Profession
दुनिया का सबसे पुराना पेशा

"Hey, Isha," said Majid, who was working on his laptop computer in their kitchen.

"Hi, honey." Aisha quietly placed her relocation guide binder down on their accent table in their entrance hall and removed her ballet flats before walking down the hallway into their kitchen. She made a quick turn to their bedroom and placed her shoes inside her hanging shoe rack that was on their closet door. She changed out of her work attire into a tank top and black spandex shorts and headed toward their kitchen.

She noticed Majid flipping through her relocation binder. Aisha ran up to him, fearing that he had seen the red-light district tab first. "Hey, babe, whatcha doin'?" She embraced him from behind but looked over his shoulders to see which tab he was reading. He looked over his left shoulder and kissed Aisha on her cheek. Aisha was relieved when she noticed him reading the food tab in the front of the binder.

"I see they created a guide book for you. That's comforting." Majid removed her hands from his waist and walked with the binder toward their sunroom.

"Uh...yeah," Aisha nervously said and walked in tow directly behind him.

As soon as he sat down on their couch, he put his feet up on their sage ottoman and smiled as he read. "I love some of the dishes they're describing in this binder—ha!—my mom used to make this for Naji and I all the time, but they spelled it wrong. Well, the food tab is OK. Let's look elsewhere..." Majid said and flipped toward the middle of the book and spotted the tab: Red-Light District. He stopped smiling and looked intently down at the photos of the females in the binder and stared at the written description of the location. "So, this is the juicy story they want you to bring back?" Majid said, noticing Aisha's eyes widening as she looked on with him.

"I tried to tell you..." Aisha glimpsed down, almost ashamed that she had not provided all of the details of the assignment.

"So they want you to come back with a story on women who sell their bodies. How are you supposed to get that story? By selling yours?" Majid looked defiantly at Aisha and then continued to read about the dangers in that area. He rested his chin on his hand and rubbed his goatee as he read a paragraph here and there.

He started to laugh nervously and then flipped pages until he got to Cyndi Jenkins's photograph. Cyndi was sitting down, wearing a transparent orange veil on her head, and henna dye was in between her black eyebrows. She had her hands resting on her thighs. She wore a midriff red top and a long skirt that was red with orange designs. He also noticed her hand decorated with henna up to her forearm. "So is this supposed to be your look over there? And when did you take this photograph?" Majid asked, looking nastily at Aisha.

Aisha shook her head and slowly removed the binder from Majid and got on top of his lap, facing him. He breathed deeply and sat back farther on the couch. She said, "Give me a chance to explain. First of all, I am not going to India to sell anything, and you should know better than that. Second, you're right. Apparently, there is a story in this particular area; I am under strict orders from my boss that I have to uncover a mysterious woman's past that involved the red-light district. Lastly, that woman in the picture is not me." Aisha turned around to remove the photo from the binder and held it next to her face for Majid to see.

Majid's eyes looked at the photo and then at Aisha several times. "It looks like you." He was about to move Aisha from off of him.

"No, sweetheart, look closer. I found something that is distinguishable between me and Cyndi. She has a tiny mole directly underneath her left eye; I do not. See—look again!" Aisha forcefully shoved the photo closer to Majid's eyes and placed her face closer to his as well.

Majid cleaned his reading glasses and looked again. He breathed slowly and finally nodded his head to Aisha that he believed her.

Aisha relaxed a little. "And not only that as proof, but this." She turned over the copy of the photo and showed the date the photo was taken: November 11, 1993.

Majid relaxed his body more on the couch; he removed his glasses again to rub his eyelids and placed them back on. "You're right. So who is she, why does she look like you, and what do you need with her in Kolkata?" Majid asked, moving Aisha from his legs.

She helped him by reluctantly getting up and then sitting down on the couch beside him. "Her name is Cyndi Jenkins. She was a journalist in the States for many years. Last year *Hartford Journal* bought the paper she used to work for. Larry, my boss, discovered this story through another journalist, Lydia, who relocated to Kolkata years ago on assignment. She found Cyndi's photograph in one of the brothels, I believe." Aisha stopped to look at her man. He was staring at her intently, waiting for her to continue. "Lydia noticed the photograph and took it to the consulate," Aisha concluded.

"You mean she stole it. If she did not ask these women if she could have it, then it was stolen. She went to an area of the world she knew nothing about and thought it would be cool to take something that probably should not have been touched," Majid said sternly.

Aisha nodded but continued her story. "When she brought it back to the States, we found out Cyndi Jenkins was an American who was on assignment there but never returned to the US. Lydia failed the assignment because she damaged her relationship with the local women of the area due to her stealing the photograph. The *Hartford Journal* thought it best to send someone from a darker persuasion over there to make peace with the people and to find out more about Cyndi Jenkins's whereabouts but to also complete what Lydia started. These brothels have teenage girls working in them—" Aisha stopped talking when Majid put up his hand indicating he heard enough.

"So your white American boss wants you to go over to Kolkata to expose a piece of India, but a bad piece of it. That's real smart of you, Aisha, to sign up willingly for this," Majid said, crossing his arms.

"I did not sign up for this; I was more like *chosen* for this. Babe, my job is resting on this assignment. I will have consulate protection and also a Bengali Consulate translator with me when I visit the brothels. You showed me a couple of days ago what it's like being a Khan. I am now showing you what it's like being the significant other of a journalist. We travel and sometimes have to go to exotic places and become investigators for stories. I promise the story I bring back will show the good and bad of this area. I know what you mean. I am not going to be a *Sambo* and bring back a story bad-mouthing this region. I plan on telling the truth, my truth, as I see it with my own two eyes."

She caressed Majid's hand. "How can I bad-mouth a people that I plan on marrying? It doesn't work that way. America has prostitution. It is the world's oldest profession, not just one country's. I am not going to get supercilious and write a story that pretends it just goes on in Kolkata. I am going to be as non-biased as possible. I can only imagine your family reading my story once I bring it back. So I know I better, and I'll err on the less explicit side and write this story from a more transparent place, illustrating the complexities of human behavior," she concluded.

Majid shook his head and picked up the photograph and noticed the Hindi script below the woman's portrait. He laughed and slightly shook the photo at Aisha. "Black gold: that's who she is there. This story just keeps getting funnier, and what are you? Little black gold?" Majid asked sarcastically.

Aisha removed the photo from Majid's hands and slapped him across the face. "Well, my black gold got you, didn't it!" Aisha bellowed and stood over him.

Majid shook his head abruptly from feeling the slap, and he laughed at Aisha's comment. "Touché, Ms. Benson."

She crossed her arms in front of her chest. "I didn't deserve that. My job depends on this assignment. I know they are setting me up for what appears to be a shady story, but like I said, that's not what I'll bring back." Aisha sat back down on the couch, continuing to keep her arms crossed.

Majid's right cheek turned bright red from her slap. He touched the right side of his face, clenched his jaw, and picked the binder back up to read the additional tabs. Aisha felt bad for hitting him across the face and moved closer to try and hug her man.

"Back up, Isha. I gotta process what they are asking my lady to do. I'm going to read this over, and you're going to give me some space." Majid's voice grew deeper as he spoke sternly.

Aisha did not get the point and continued to stare with a concerned look at Majid. He slammed his hand down on the binder and shot her a look that showed her he wanted her to leave the room.

Aisha left the room to prepare their dinner.

The two lay separate from one another in their bed after dinner, absorbed in their own thoughts. Aisha was on the left side of their bed, and Majid was on the right. They had never realized how big their queen-size bed was, since they had always held each other before going to sleep.

Majid kept turning in his sleep, and Aisha continued to wake up because of it. She slowly glided her way over to Majid. She gently massaged her foot on top of his left foot.

Majid opened his eyes and smiled. He returned her gentle touch and rubbed his foot as well. "Come here." Majid pulled Aisha into him and carressed her arms underneath the covers. "Come back safely to me, baby girl; that's an order. Your boss gave you orders, and now I'm giving you mine," Majid whispered into her ear and kissed her neck.

Aisha felt relieved that he was OK with it. "That's the only way I plan on coming back. I'll bring *Sally* with me just in case somebody gets tricky," Aisha said, caressing Majid's face.

Majid chuckled. "You don't need your taser gun. Just hit them with your right hook; didn't know you had it in you, Isha." Majid moved his tongue toward the right side of his mouth. "I tasted blood after you hit me. That's when I realized you could take care of yourself, but part of me still wishes I could be there to protect you, though." He squeezed her tighter.

"Sorry, babe. You got sassy with me, so I had to let you know," Aisha said, giggling, but then she stroked the area of his face she hit.

"What was Chris Rock's joke years ago? A man can't hit back? All I can do is shake you—someth'n like that." Majid playfully shook Aisha's shoulders.

"I'm sorry, babe," she said, laughing.

"Don't be. I was reacting to what could possibly happen, forgetting how smart you are and brave; I love you, Isha." Majid stroked her hair, which removed the concerned look from her face. He playfully rubbed his nose on the side of her face and then kissed it.

"I love you too, Majid."

The two held each other quietly before going to sleep.

Up, Up, and Away
नर्भिय होकर आगे बढ़ो

Aisha, Majid, and the Benson family arrived at Bradley International Airport Thursday morning at six o'clock. Aisha yawned and placed her arm around Majid's shoulders. Once Majid was cool with Aisha going, she had told all of her friends and family. Aisha's mother and father decided to accompany Majid and her to the airport to send their daughter off.

"How far ahead in time are they, did you say, Majid?" Mr. Benson asked.

"Kolkata is nine and a half hours ahead, sir. The plane ride for Isha will be twenty hours long. When she gets to Kolkata it will be Friday morning there. This also includes her hour layover in Frankfurt, Germany. It will be nine p.m. our time when she arrives." Majid calculated for the family.

"Oh, well, in that case, Isha, text your mother and me once you get there, since we are old folks who go to bed early, but call Majid," Mr. Benson said.

Majid rolled Aisha's biggest suitcase toward the skycap and grabbed Aisha by the waist. "Call me as soon as you land. I don't care what time it is." He kissed her on the cheek.

"I see you've been schooled on the proper attire there, hon," Mrs. Benson said, placing another bag of Aisha's on the skycap's luggage holder.

Aisha had on a violet-colored sari, traditional Indian pants, and black ballet flats. "Yes, everyone has schooled me on the dangers if I do not, so I borrowed a couple of pieces from Chandi, my friend, and the rest I had in my closet—most were gifts from Majid." Aisha returned her boyfriend's kisses, pecking him on his cheek.

"That was the right thing to do," Mr. Benson said, weighing in.

Aisha spoke with the skycap briefly and watched as her luggage was carried away on a conveyor belt to be placed on the plane. She had her purse and laptop bag as carry-ons. The group went inside the airport and ate breakfast together at a bagel shop. Mr. Benson paid for everyone's meals. They all ate and sat close to the security checkpoint so that Aisha did not have far to walk after they were done with their meal and said their good-byes.

"So, Mr. Majid, how are the students at UCONN, brotha?" Mr. Benson said, engaging Majid.

"I am grading midterms tomorrow, so I will have a better estimation on how they are doing academically after this weekend. But I can say these students this semester do well with attendance, class participation, and group projects. The lowest grade I had to give to one group for a class project was a C. So in a classroom of sixty students, I would consider these students to be an energetic and intellectual group," Majid explained.

Mrs. Benson nodded in approval. "I love the fact that our daughter chose such a handsome and smart professor. I do not even know the first thing about biochemistry." Mrs. Benson chuckled, moving fabric from her *khimar* off the table while picking at her bagel.

"Well, growing up I had always loved science, Mrs. Benson. I was intrigued with your daughter too, once I found out what she aspired to do after college. I love the creativity she brings to her stories at the newspaper. I knew I had found someone quite unique and special when I met her," Majid said, using one hand to hold Aisha's.

"So, when Isha comes back, can she expect a ring?" Mrs. Benson provided a sly grin, sipping her tea.

Aisha looked at Majid and Majid gave a nervous laugh.

"Mr. and Mrs. Benson, I plan on taking care of that in the near future; I do not have the exact month, hour, minute, and seconds, but Aisha and I will be making an announcement in the near future. I hate that she is leaving me for three months. I am going to *miss her....*" Majid started to choke up and then clenched his fist and slightly bit the closest knuckle on his hand. After realizing he said that to her parents, he almost felt embarrassed by the passion he had behind his words.

Mr. and Mrs. Benson looked at each other with raised eyebrows. "I don't know how I feel about that type of missing you're going to experience with my daughter, young man," Mr. Benson joked.

The Bensons sat with Majid and Aisha a little longer until it was time for Aisha to go through the security checkpoint to make her flight.

"We love you, baby girl. Remember to text us and call Majid as soon as you land," Mr. Benson instructed.

She kissed her mother and father. The Bensons walked back toward the airport lobby and gave a couple of minutes to Majid to speak with Aisha alone.

Majid took her laptop bag and held her hand as he walked her a couple of feet toward the security checkpoint. They faced each other, and he caressed her cheek. "You know I am going to take care of what your mother asked, right, honey? I just need to do it in my own time. So don't come back married to another man, sweetheart. You're mine, and I am yours forever." Majid took out of his pocket a jewelry case and opened it to reveal a fourteen-carat white gold necklace with a pendant on it. "Move your hair for me," he whispered in her ear.

Aisha turned around and grabbed her hair to place on one side of her shoulder while Majid positioned the necklace around her neck. "The pendant is beautiful. What flower is this?" she asked, touching the necklace.

Majid fixed the jewelry so that the pendant dangled above her collar bone. "It's a *shapla*. This flower is the national flower of Bangladesh." He placed her computer bag on her free shoulder and brought her closer to him so that his mouth was next to her left ear. "The shapla flower is a part of the water lily family. You're my water lily, and I want you to come back to me. My mom prayed over this necklace to protect you and keep you safe. Wear it for me every day; never take it off." He playfully placed his tongue in her ear and gently circled it around the outside rim. He then kissed down her cheek until he was kissing her on the lips.

Aisha slowly parted her lips from his. "Professor Khan, I guess I didn't give you enough to calm your urges." Aisha kiddingly pushed his chest.

"It's never enough; even when we go all night." He rubbed her shoulders.

Aisha looked into his eyes, and her eyes got watery. "I have to get going. Later, my love."

Their hands slowly separated from one another, and Aisha walked away but looked back until the security gate checkpoint line blocked her view.

"*F*light eleven-ten to Frankfurt is boarding; zones three and four can now board," Aisha heard one of the flight attendants say into the microphone once she got to the gate.

She looked down at her boarding pass and noticed that she was in zone three. "Of course *Hartford Journal* was too cheap to get me first class," she said out loud.

The flight attendant scanned her ticket, and Aisha boarded the plane. The huge aircraft offered plenty of room between seats. She was thankful when she noticed her seat was closest to the aisle. She placed her laptop in one of the overhead compartments and then sat down. She observed how she was the only African American on the flight, while most were Indian, and a few were Caucasian. Some of the Indians noticed her attire and smiled at her with a slight chuckle. She smiled back and shared her seating row with an Indian couple who had their child.

The mother had the child on her lap and saw Aisha smiling at her baby. "Don't worry. I fed him already, and this is his second trip to Germany. He may cry at times, but for the most part, he is a quiet baby," she said, rocking him back and forth. The baby's eyes closed slightly. The husband looked down at his child and then out the seat row's window.

Aisha went into her purse and pulled out her cell phone. She noticed a couple of "safe flight" text messages from Majid's aunts. Kelsey, her co-worker, also wished her a safe flight. Nivritti Yadav, her interpreter, sent a text saying, "See you on the other side; call me when you get here. I have your itinerary and will meet you at the airport. Up, Up, and Away..." Nivritti had included a bird icon at the end of her sentence.

She's got a sense of humor, Aisha thought and smiled. She turned off her cell phone and closed her eyes.

The flight attendant spoke into the microphone. "Passengers, welcome aboard flight ten-ten to Frankfurt, Germany. We will be in flight for seven hours, with a connecting flight for those going to Kolkata, India, as the final destination. First-class passengers will choose from an assortment of entrees for breakfast, lunch, and dinner. For our coach passengers, for lunch and dinner we offer ham, turkey, or beef sandwiches and also a salad for vegetarian passengers. For breakfast you will have a choice of a bagel or fruit cup. Alcoholic beverages will be served; we accept all major credit cards. At this time please turn off all gadgets; this includes iPods, cell phones, and tablets. Our flight attendants are currently walking around to make sure your seat is upright. We will let you know when it is safe to turn on electronic devices again. The current weather in Germany is fifty-seven degrees and cloudy. Again, welcome aboard. Flight attendants, prepare for takeoff."

Aisha turned her face to her right side to look out the window as the plane picked up speed to go up in the air. She turned her head back to the seat in front of her and closed her eyes as the plane gently shook, catching speed before takeoff. She allowed her mind to wander. In her meditative state, she swore she heard Majid's voice in her head—*Come back safely, baby girl*—and it brought a smile to her face. She envisioned kissing him on the lips and imagined whispering in his ear, "I'm going up, up, and away."

Welcome to Kolkata
कोलकाता में आपका स्वागत है

Aisha felt like she was being slightly pushed in her seat. She turned toward her left and noticed another Indian family that was next to her from her flight from Frankfurt to Kolkata. Their child was the polar opposite of the other child she had been on the first flight with. This child's feet were nudging her in the arm. The baby's eyes were big, filled with curiosity, adventure, and playfulness. He had constantly whimpered on the plane during the flight and hardly slept. Aisha smiled and removed the blanket from her shoulder. The mother of the child smiled at Aisha and rocked her baby back and forth.

"Ladies and gentlemen, we've arrived in Kolkata. Please return your seats back to their original position, and seat trays should be placed back up. The time here is six thirty a.m., and the current temperature is seventy degrees, with cloudy skies. We hope your stay in Kolkata is enjoyable. Flight attendants, prepare for landing."

As the plane landed in a bumpy fashion, slightly swaying the passengers, Aisha immediately snatched her cell phone out of her purse and turned it on. She was so excited to call Majid but text messaged her parents first and decided to wait to call Majid once she got situated in her hotel. Once the plane arrived at the terminal, Aisha and the Indian family next to her both sighed in unison. This had been the longest she had traveled to a destination. Aisha had spent her leisure time walking around the cabin or reading a book to make the time go by; she also rested as best as she could.

She grabbed her laptop out of the carry-on plane compartment and filed in line to get off the plane. Once Aisha was inside the airport, she looked around. The airport was bustling with energy. Tons of people were strolling around as she looked for signs directing people to baggage claim. She saw the sign and began walking. The airport was huge. She saw a sign with writing that said, "Welcome to Kolkata," and she noticed another standing sign that described where she was located: the airport's new terminal.

This has to be the new terminal, as I've been told some other areas in the airport are not as clean, she thought. She got on the escalator that headed to ground level to baggage claim to pick up her two suitcases. Once she got them, she checked her phone to see if Nivritti had text messaged her. She saw one new message and read it:

> I am standing outside of the Air India gate under the sign, I-16. I have on a dark green sari. Let's see if we can find one another among the chaos. See you soon. N. Y.

Aisha giggled at the message and walked outside of the airport. She was at gate entrance I-12 and began walking down to the sixteenth gate. She heard honking horns and noticed trash was along the walkway. She tried her best to pay attention to what she was stepping in, as she saw food haphazardly discarded along her path. She got to the sixteenth gate and noticed who she believed to be Nivritti. The woman looked at her as well. She had on a dark green sari, and her hair was neatly braided down her back.

She offered a warm smile to Aisha as they walked toward one another. "Welcome to Kolkata, Shadow." Nivritti nodded her head and winked.

"Thank you. I am looking forward to it," Aisha said, gazing around the airport.

"You must be ready to head to the hotel. Come. I got us a taxi. The driver may not be the most pleasant; we've been waiting now for an hour." Nivritti hustled Aisha to the taxi.

"Sorry..." Aisha said halfheartedly, placing her suitcases in the trunk of the taxi.

"Don't be. Consulate paid for the taxi. He's been getting paid this entire time," Nivritti said. She spoke to the taxi driver in Hindi, and he reluctantly smiled at Aisha and pulled off from the airport. "This is the safest way for you to travel through Kolkata, Shadow. Always look for the yellow taxi cab. The hotel you're staying at, Broadway Hotel, has a place where you can convert your US dollars into Indian rupees. Make sure you always jot down what you paid for travel so that your company can reimburse you. You will find the dollar goes a long way here. For instance, the cost of the airport to the city center, where your hotel is, costs three hundred rupees." Nivritti said.

Aisha's eyes widened.

"Yeah, it sounds like a lot. But guess what that means in US dollars? Close to around a mere five dollars." She noticed Aisha's surprised reaction. Nivritti smiled and nodded. "See, your American money goes far here."

Aisha looked out the window of the taxi, beginning to get comfortable with her ride through the town center. Suddenly, the taxi began to swerve and jerk rapidly. Aisha noticed tons of people walking or riding their bicycles on both sides of the taxi. She began to get uncomfortable, watching closely to how the taxi driver was navigating. She opened her mouth and gasped each time he nearly hit someone. Aisha, realizing he would not be able to understand her, looked over at Nivritti. Nivritti was sitting back comfortably in the seat with her legs crossed, appearing unfazed and looking rather regal. Aisha kept looking at Nivritti, waiting for a normal reaction to the taxi driver's style of driving.

Nivritti turned her head toward Aisha's direction, looking confused. "What's wrong?" she asked her.

Aisha laughed and shook her head. "Uh, do you not notice his driving?" she said sarcastically.

Nivritti made a "who cares" hand gesture. "You're in Kolkata, dear; this is how we drive here, especially the taxis. Isn't where you lived in Connecticut close to New York City? I've heard your taxi drivers are not much different," Nivritti challenged.

"Um...Connecticut is obviously not close enough, because I would be like you and not care that he looks to be on the verge of killing people. So where did you go to college in the US?" Aisha asked, changing the subject.

"I attended Princeton and graduated summa cum laude, with a major in International Affairs." The sentence rolled off of Nivritti's tongue as if she'd been waiting for Aisha to ask for her life story. "After graduating, I stayed in the US for four years, working at Princeton for a year and a half, assisting in one of their departments—Research Program in Political Economy. It's a fascinating research studies program; it bridges the gaps between the study disciplines of political science and economics."

Aisha began to roll her eyes at the gloating Nivritti was doing.

As Nivritti talked, she kept looking down at her wedding ring and French manicured nails, not paying the slightest attention to Aisha's disinterest. "My focus in the department was assisting with providing grants to students to continue their research in political economy, which means them taking short-term visits to different universities throughout the States and abroad as well as meeting with worldly scholars on international affairs. However, I realized working there did not provide the fulfillment I had enjoyed as a student, so I gracefully left and accepted another position, working as a foreign services officer for the United States. I was able to visit my homeland again here in Kolkata, and I traveled throughout Asia, specifically China, for ten months." Nivritti, at this time, had a reminiscent look and patted her braid before pushing it behind her shoulder.

Aisha couldn't believe how self-aggrandizing Nivritti was. She was trying to figure out a way to show Nivritti she was done hearing about her accomplishments.

"When I went to China, I visited the Great Wall. I'll show you photos, darling. No worries." Nivritti swayed her fingers back and forth as if she were allowing her perfectly polished nails to air-dry. "I even got to learn a little Manda—"

Nivritti stopped speaking immediately when she heard Aisha on the other side of the seat, pretending to snore—and doing so loudly.

"Ugh..." Nivritti flipped her braid in Aisha's direction and stopped talking to look out of the window.

Aisha, peeking out of the corner of her left eye, noticed that Nivritti had gotten the point to stop talking. She grinned in happy silence all the way to the Broadway Hotel.

Aisha got out of the taxi cab, happy that she had enjoyed five minutes or so of silence. As she removed her luggage from the cab, Nivritti spoke to the driver and passed him payment for the fare. He looked to be flirting with Nivritti and gave Nivritti back some of the money. Aisha watched the display between the two of them and waited on the top step of the hotel for Nivritti to join her. Aisha left one of her suitcases on the step.

"Shadow, darling, you forgot a suitcase, dear," Nivritti said, indicating with her head that she was not there to assist Aisha with her luggage.

Aisha narrowed her eyes, walked back over to the top step, snatched her suitcase, removed a long piece of her hair from underneath her *khimar*, and flipped her hair at Nivritti. She looked Nivritti up and down and said, "And it's all real too, boo."

Nivritti smiled and laughed. "Let's get your hotel key for your new home," Nivritti said, walking past Aisha to the concierge's desk. Nivritti spoke in fluent Hindi to the concierge, who was rather candid with her in conversation.

After about ten minutes, Nivritti tapped Aisha on the shoulders and held her hand out. "Corporate card, dear. They gave you a deal as well. I told them you were a celebrity journalist, like the equivalent of Soledad O'Brien." Nivritti winked.

Aisha shook her head in laughter and provided her corporate card to Nivritti.

"Good, it's a Visa. Just so you know, most places here only accept Visa or MasterCard," Nivritti said as she handed the concierge the card.

Aisha looked around and noticed another desk, where she watched a man convert his dollars into rupees. "Hey, girl, I'm going to convert some of my dollars. I'll be right back," Aisha said and proceeded to walk away, leaving her luggage with Nivritti.

"Shadow, come back right after. I'm not here to help you with your luggage!" Nivritti yelled toward the other side of the hotel lobby in Aisha's direction.

The two women got to Aisha's new digs and unlocked the door. The room had two double beds; both had very thin mattresses. Aisha noticed a TV across from the beds and then walked inside of the bathroom. It was a basic bathroom with a toilet and quaint shower. She reluctantly rolled her luggage over to the other side of the room and looked around, confused. "This is it?" Aisha asked, unimpressed.

"Now who's being the diva?" Nivritti said, crossing her arms. "You know, your company picked one of the best hotels in Kolkata; be grateful, dear." As she sat on one of the beds, Nivritti said in a much lower voice, "Besides, after what you're going to see on this trip, you'll be blessed to come back here."

Aisha heard what she said but chose to switch the subject. "So, how did you meet Lydia, the woman that was on assignment here years ago?" Aisha asked, beginning to unpack some of her luggage.

"It was the year I came back to live in Kolkata and the year I got married." Nivritti's eyes sparkled as she looked down at her ring. "You know, my husband works in international affairs as well; he travels the world and is from London. He was the one Lydia befriended. She handed him the photo at the consulate of you-know-who..." Nivritti said.

"Who? Black Gold?" Aisha asked.

"Right. Exactly...So I see they gave you a binder about Kolkata?" Nivritti asked, moving toward Aisha's suitcase and looking in it. She removed the binder and perused through it before picking up a sari from Aisha's suitcase.

"Why are you so uncomfortable speaking about her?" Aisha asked, playfully removing the sari shirt from Nivritti's hands.

"You know, you look so much like her—well, when she was around your age, that is. Now she is Black *Antique* Gold," Nivritti said, laughing.

Aisha laughed as well at the comment. "So have you seen her?" Aisha asked, removing a hanger from the hotel room closet.

"No, she would never be in the red-light district. She is above that place now and has been for years…" Nivritti said, scratching her head uncomfortably.

"Well, what does that mean? I thought she was like the queen of the red-light district," Aisha probed.

"The queen—funny. Well, if there is anything higher than a queen, you can best believe she is that now. She is kept encased in Hari Vishnu's compound. She rarely speaks to anyone, but I have a feeling she will speak to you. What I have heard about her is that she does make visits to the district, but she is protected with tons of Vishnu's men. She is kind of like a celebrity in the red-light district. There hasn't been talk about her for a while though. For all I know, she could be dead. What she did for those children…" Nivritti trailed off for a few moments before bringing her focus back to Aisha.

"What? Tell me more about her. I'll have to know eventually. I only have three months here, so I can't joyride the experience entirely. I'm going to have to eventually get to work," Aisha said, sitting down now across from Nivritti on the other bed.

"You have plenty of time to learn about Black Gold, but enough of her for today. Let's see. It's nine thirty a.m. How about I take you over to the Blue Sky Café on Sudder Street for some breakfast? And then we can head to the Indian Museum." Nivritti clasped her hands together in excitement.

After hearing Nivritti provide the time, Aisha frantically looked into her purse for her phone. "Oh my goodness. It must be like midnight in the US. Nivritti, I am all for hanging out with you today, but let's meet up again in the afternoon, say around three p.m. I desperately need some sleep, and I must call my boyfriend. He must be so worried now." Aisha looked at her phone and noticed six missed calls from Majid.

"Got it. I can see by the bags underneath your eyes how tired you are," Nivritti said, nonchalantly sticking her tongue out.

"Excuse me?" Aisha asked, looking over to Nivritti, who was leaving her room.

"Text me later. Enjoy your sleep and husband. He should have gotten you a ring, you know." Nivritti sent a passing wave over to Aisha and left her room.

Aisha rolled her eyes and thumbed through her cell phone to call Majid.

He answered on the third ring. "Hello," Majid said with a groggy voice into the phone.

Aisha couldn't help but lick her lips at the sound of her man's voice. His voice always turned her on when it was at its deepest tone. "Hey, love, sorry to call you so late," she said into the phone, placing the Do not Disturb sign on the outside of the door before locking it. She walked over to the bed area and moved some clothes she had out onto the other bed and sprawled her body onto the mattress, twirling her hair.

"Baby girl, I'm glad you called me back. I was getting worried. I thought our cell phone carrier did not set up your global package correctly and that you may have needed a calling card or something, so I did not trip out. Plus, I also spoke to your parents; so I knew you landed safely. I miss holding you in bed," Majid said, yawning into the phone.

Aisha smiled and removed her clothes until she got down to her undergarments and then slid underneath the sheets. "You sound so sexy, honey. Let me guess what you have on: a black undershirt and gray boxers," she said, biting her finger.

"Not even close, darling. I have on blue pajama pants and no shirt, and I just placed on my reading glasses so I can write down the address of the hotel you're staying at. You must of forgotten to leave that information for me," Majid said sternly.

"Oh, you have on the reading glasses, mmm, hmm." Aisha's mind was in another place, picturing Majid just as he described himself.

"We'll get to that, beloved, but I need the address first."

Aisha heard him tapping a pen on his nightstand. "I'm staying at the Broadway Hotel on Twenty-Seven-A Ganesh Chandra Avenue, zip code 700 013...you know the rest." She heard him writing it down.

"Got it. How was your flight?" Majid asked as Aisha heard him place the pen on his nightstand. She heard him switch on the lamp on top of his nightstand and adjust his body to sit up on the bed.

"The flights were long. Frankfurt felt like the temperature back in Connecticut at fifty-seven degrees. The highlight of my layover was that I ate some tasty German food at a restaurant while I was at the airport. A dish called *tafelspitz*—the waitress explained to me that they boil the beef in a broth, and it is commonly served with horseradish. She also explained that it really is Austrian, but the state, Bavaria, is so close to Austria that it eventually spread through Germany. I also got us a German shot glass souvenir as well. You know I always get one of those no matter where we go. Once I ate and walked around the airport, the hour layover did not seem as long. The flight from Frankfurt to Kolkata was a bit turbulent; we went through a storm. But guess what? I held on to my necklace. My *shapla* kept me safe, and I eventually fell asleep. I woke up from getting kicked by a baby's little feet and heard a flight attendant on the loudspeaker say that we arrived in Kolkata." The two of them grew silent on the phone as Aisha pictured Majid nodding his head, taking in her travel story.

"What's your interpreter, Nivritti, like?" he asked.

Aisha rolled her eyes and began to describe her. "We're getting used to each other: feeling each other out as women do. She was there on time. In fact, she told me she and the taxi driver were waiting an hour for me. I do not know why they waited so long, since she had my trip itinerary beforehand and the flight landed on time," she said.

"It's our culture. We would think it bad manners to have someone waiting on us who is foreign to our country and looking for us to be their tour guide, so to speak; first impressions are a big deal to us. What do you mean about getting used to each other?" he asked with dirty thoughts flirting around in his head.

"Well, I was trying to hold a light, bubbly conversation with her in the taxi ride from the airport to the hotel, so I asked her about her career and education. Don't you know home girl gave me such a snooty story about her schooling and accomplishments," Aisha told Majid.

"Don't take that personally, Ish. Indians are very proud of their education; we hold it to a very high standard. We come from a very poor country; you're going to see that about India. It's almost a country that belongs in a different time period—very mystical in some respects but also a torn country. It has beautiful, sacred temples that have been somewhat preserved. When I think about it, India is a contradiction of itself. On a street with a sacred temple, it's not uncommon to find people running scams on tourists and for the street to be filled with litter. The Hindu temples are pristine inside because we respect our ancestors, but once you get outside, you will see present-day Indians, and some of the habits we have are not so good. This is true for people everywhere, though, especially when you travel outside of the United States. For Americans, poor is not having the latest fashions and technology. For other countries, poor is not having running water or not having an efficient sewage system. But the country is changing, and we have pockets of advanced business districts, so you're seeing a lot and will probably come back to the States and feel blessed to be from America."

Aisha was quiet, reflecting on what she heard Majid say.

"So how does she look? You all checked each other out?" Majid asked jokingly.

"Shut up, boy! She's very regal and attractive. She's married; she kept flaunting her ring in my face," Aisha pouted into the phone.

"I'm sure you're being paranoid, Isha. She was not flaunting her ring in your face. Indian women are taught that they are princesses from the time they're young girls; I'm sure she has an air, so to speak, but in terms of attitude, I don't think Indian women are much different than black women: you both have feisty attitudes. That's why I was never intimidated by you when were first started dating; it was appealing to me," Majid said seductively. "So you two are keeping each other company?" he asked. Aisha heard him licking his lips.

"You are so nasty! No, I sent her on her way. I told her I was tired and called you; we're meeting up later, after I get some sleep."

Majid started laughing. "Just playing, sweetheart. I only have eyes for you, baby, but my mind does wander after midnight, and it's going to get worse now that you're not here with me physically."

Aisha could almost picture Majid grinning into the phone. She grew tired of discussing her travels and puckered her lips and placed her right hand onto her stomach, looking to steer the conversation back to her and Majid only. "Let's take advantage of your dirty thoughts...You know, one of my hands is gently caressing a part of my body that's a favorite feature of yours. Guess which part I'm talking about?" Aisha alluringly asked.

"Mmm, hmm, there are so many areas. Your body is my playground. I'm game for a little phone sex, since this is the only way I'm gonna be gett'n any for the next ninety days," Majid said frustratingly, looking at a hanging calendar on their wall. "But if I were there, I'd start with caressing your neck slowly," Majid whispered into the phone.

Aisha removed her hand from her stomach and brought it up to her neck, making caressing strokes. "What would you do after that?" she asked him.

"I would kiss and lick your neck sensuously, just the way you like it. I know it drives you crazy," he said, his voice getting deeper.

Aisha closed her eyes, allowing herself to be entranced by his voice and imagining his sweet kisses. "Where would you explore next?" she probed.

"I would take my kisses and make a trail with my tongue down to your stomach and gently bite you, hearing you moan in pleasure. And before I get to my favorite place in the world, I would tease you by biting your thighs."

Aisha bit her lips and placed her hand on her thighs, rubbing them first slowly and then feverishly.

Majid could almost picture her movements being manipulated by his voice, and he continued, "I'd get to your feet and rub them softly and slowly after I explored your coffee-complexioned legs."

Aisha imagined Majid in front of her, grabbing her leg and placing it on his chest, proceeding to play with her toe rings and lightly sucking her toes as only he could do to make her body quiver. "Ooh, Professor Khan, I've had enough—I can't let you tease me anymore...Guess where your hand is now?" She started to make kissing and moaning noises into the phone.

Majid heard Aisha continuing to whimper and softly utter his name, breathing very deeply until finally releasing high-pitched groans.

She heard him lick his lips into the phone as he asked in a calm, concentrated voice, "Dang Isha *my* hands are already there? Mmm, mmm, that's *my* girl..."

The Tourist Experience
पर्यटक का अनुभव

Nivritti and Aisha met up at 4:30 p.m. on Sudder Street at the Blue Sky Café restaurant. After their lunch, they walked the streets as Nivritti narrated pieces of Kolkata's history. They entered the Indian Museum, only paying the equivalent of $2.75 in US dollars each.

Aisha was stunned by the beauty of the museum around Park Street, where it was located. "My boyfriend was right. It's amazing how the streets look so clean once we get to a landmark," she said. She had on a sari and jean pants with ballet flats.

"Yeah, West Bengal is like that. You will find some streets where the landmarks are almost frozen in time because they are so ancient. And we keep it that way. A few of us are Hindu. Are you Baptist?" Nivritti asked, allowing Aisha to first step through a vestibule of the Art Gallery in the museum.

"No, I know it is very common for African Americans to be Baptist, but my family is actually Muslim," Aisha said.

"That's interesting. Yeah, I saw some *khimars* in your suitcase. So do you not practice?" Nivritti asked, admiring a bust of the Hindu goddess Lakshmi.

"Well, I am sort of on the fence when it comes to Islam. My boyfriend is Muslim as well; his family is from Dhaka," Aisha said looking at the Hindu goddess.

"Oh, so you're into Asian men too, like Black Gold, I see?" Nivritti grabbed her chest and laughed.

Aisha ignored the comment and admired the bust and the jewelry that adorned the Hindu goddess. She touched the glass that encased the piece just as a glimmer of light glistened over the both of them. The light had a subtleness to it: if you blinked, you would have missed it.

Nivritti looked from the bust to Aisha and arched her eyebrows. "Interesting. Shadow, just as a piece of advice: you do not want to mess with the gods here. Be mindful of your thoughts, as they tend to manifest very quickly in Kolkata. Perhaps, though, your luck is changing for you. Lakshmi represents wealth and prosperity, both material and spiritual. I dare say she took a liking to you. The gods can see people's spirits for what they truly are… Let's move on."

Nivritti slightly bowed her head, and Aisha mimicked as well before walking toward another piece of artwork.

"So how long have you been dating this man from Dhaka?" she asked, beginning to soften to Aisha.

"We've been together for nine years. We bumped into each other on the Yale campus. I was attending school there, and he was there for a teacher's conference," Aisha answered.

"You went to Yale? How brilliant! You're an extraordinary woman. So he is a professor?" she asked.

"Yep, my boo is a recently tenured biochemistry professor for the University of Connecticut. Huskies all day long!" Aisha made a hand gesture to acknowledge UCONN's mascot.

Nivritti looked confused and laughed at Aisha's gesture.

"Girl, loosen up! Don't you ever just chill? You know you can be smart without being so stuffy. Bet you didn't think I was an alum of an Ivy League school," Aisha challenged.

"Well, I did not know what to think. I did not think you were dumb or anything, but you know…" Nivritti trailed off.

Aisha narrowed her eyes at Nivritti. "Anyway, I'm going to ignore your comment because I need you for this trip. This museum has peacefulness to it. Do most landmarks in Kolkata expect lots of silence while visiting them?" she asked.

"Indian people respect their temples and landmarks, as they are preserved places, so the short answer is yes," Nivritti affirmed.

The women talked some more. Nivritti became very impressed with Aisha's education and accomplishments. They entered the Musical Instrument Gallery and took in the beauty of artifacts that were encased.

"You know, Shadow, I can't help but to notice your necklace; it's beautiful. He gave that to you, didn't he?" Nivritti asked as they approached an ancient Hindi musical score.

Aisha was surprised how intuitive Nivritti was. "Yeah…How did you know?" she asked.

"When a woman is in love, she carries herself differently. I can't seem to take my eyes off of it. It glows with your affection for one another," Nivritti said, touching her hair, seeming to be uncomfortable with how she could see into Aisha's life this way.

"His mother blessed the necklace too. You know, Majid was not cool with this assignment. Coming over here to work on the story was troubling for him, but he loves me and trusts me," Aisha concluded.

"Oh, there is love, very deep and intense. Do not take off the necklace. If his mother blessed it for the purpose of protection, you must wear it at all times then. You don't want to worry him. He can feel you even when you're not close to him," she said.

"It's amusing that you said that, because I sometimes think I can hear him speaking to me. You know, he and I have this thing where we can have the same dream at night; it's kind of funny," Aisha shared.

"You all are very connected to each other; that's quite special." Nivritti looked down to read about the encased Hindi musical score. "*Chanda Sutra* was created by Indian scholar Pingala; this is a Sanskrit poem. A lot of Indian musical scores were first poems, you know. Oh, cool, they have inscribed on this piece the seven basic pitches of a musical scale. You know, like in America you have do, re, mi, fa, so, la, ti. We have sa, re, ga, ma, pa, dha, ni." Nivritti recited the scale in a harmonized pitch.

"You have a pretty voice. Are you a singer too?" Aisha asked.

"I grew up in a musical family. I studied a little on American music, and I learned quite a lot about black Americans and their love of music too. I enjoy rhythm and blues, as you all call it, right?" Nivritti asked.

"Yeah, you said it long-winded; we call it R&B," Aisha explained.

"My family loved Tagore songs. Tagore was a man from here and wrote beautiful poetry and music. His music is celebrated all over West Bengal. I developed my voice from vocal training with my mother, who was a talented singer as well," she said.

"Why did you not pursue music for your career?" Aisha asked.

"In my family, music is respected, but it is not a field the Yadav family thinks is worth boasting about. Most Indian people are musically inclined as well as intrinsic dancers, like black people. So in my family, we have the talent, but how does it help people? Don't get me wrong: music can be healing, but I did not develop the talent enough to where I could be the next Tagore. I have three brothers who are doctors, and I am the youngest and female. When my parents noticed my passion to help people, they wanted me to pursue medicine like my brothers, but that's not what I wanted. I wanted to help people in another way, and once I got accepted to an American university to study international affairs, they found something to brag about when it came to their only daughter," she concluded.

"So, *Chandra Sutra*—is that kind of like the *Kama Sutra*?" Aisha asked, swaying her hips in a provocative manner.

Nivritti's eyes got wide, and she placed her hands on Aisha's shoulders. *"O Mere Bhagwan,* no!" Nivritti scolded her. "I thought you were Muslim? Aren't Muslim women conservative?"

Aisha laughed but then remembered all of her family and friends who warned her about Kolkata's beliefs of how a woman should conduct themselves in public. "Sorry, jeez. I do not see anyone else around us; I'm just having fun. Majid and I are very liberal Muslims—well, behind closed doors, anyways. He loves when I sway my hips for him." Aisha joked to Nivritti.

"It looked like you know how to do some belly dancing too," Nivritti said, observing.

"I never actually took a belly dancing class before, so, nope, I guess it just kind of comes from within," Aisha said.

"I can teach you a few things. Indians are not frigid people, but there is a time and place for everything. You Americans and your fascination with the *Kama Sutra*," Nivritti said, shaking her head. "The book explores more than sexual positions. Before reading that book, I encourage every American to see sexuality different than what they have been conditioned to," Nivritti said.

"Well, what do you mean?" Aisha asked.

Nivritti looked around the museum for a seat. "Come, let's relax for a second. I am getting tired of walking."

The two walked into the Archaeology Section of the museum and found a bench to sit on.

"Americans tend to pervert the body. Sex is a very spiritual and sacred act. Yes, it's pleasurable, but our gods tell us sex can be used for other things. You can draw inspiration from sex; that's why it is so important to choose your partners carefully. People who are strongly compatible manifest remarkable accomplishments in life. The *Kama Sutra* has chapters on the attainment of knowledge, priorities in life, the union of marriage, and the four main goals according to the author, Vātsyāyana: dharma, artha, kama, and moksha. To break it down, *dharma* means righteous living, *artha* means material affluence, *kama* means beauty and erotic satisfaction, and, finally, *moksha* means autonomy. What did not get translated clearly in my opinion from the book is the importance it places on living an honorable life so that you can stop the cycle of rebirth and finally become one with the source. Pleasure seeking should be of least importance the older we get. The book explains the dangers of enjoying the senses. Two lovers blinded by their own passions can lead a very perilous life.

"Work on developing the higher chakras, not the lower ones. Look at the lower ones as gifts to not be used frivolously. They aid in your understanding of life and connect you to your partner, but the book is not Tantric in nature; many Americans mistake it for that. Tantric practice is really Buddhist but has influenced some Hindus. Meeting the right person, the person you connect the most with in life, is important. If you all are blessed to find each other, your lives will be very blissful, and you all can be crucial to the progress of humanity by what you create together. There are seasons where you and your partner should practice sex to produce the type of child you want: intellectual, spiritual—it's very mystical. This is the true understanding of the *Kama Sutra*."

"Yikes, you said a mouthful; Professor Yadav is in the building," Aisha said, pretending to curtsy to her.

"There is still so much to see. Let's run through the museum a little more before we head out." Nivritti got up from the bench, and Aisha followed in tow.

The two of them walked around the museum more before heading out. They came up to Sudder Street again, which was a couple of streets over from Aisha's hotel on Ganesh Chandra Avenue. She and Nivritti walked the entire museum and wanted to rest. They came up to a man who was on the street, smoking, and beside him was a rickshaw.

"I think you should experience this at least once," Nivritti said as she pulled Aisha by the hand. *"Kripya hame Ganesh Chandra Avenue le chale,"* Nivritti said to the driver.

He looked the two of them up and down and flicked his cigarette into a dirty puddle. He glanced back at Nivritti and helped both women into the rickshaw. Nivritti, with perfect posture, crossed one leg over the other and looked around Sudder Street. Aisha slightly caved in her torso and looked around, hoping no one was staring at the two of them.

"What's your issue?" Nivritti asked, noticing Aisha's body language.

"I don't like this, girl. I feel like this is degrading for people who make a living doing this; that's all," Aisha said.

"The population of Kolkata is around five million the last time I checked. Many people here do not have access to the best education, and therefore employment will be limited based on that. This man is providing for himself and his family the best way he can; you should not feel bad. Give him American money when we get off, and see how happy he gets," she said, winking her eye.

The human rickshaw slowly made his way with the women to Ganesh Chandra Avenue. He stopped and placed the handles on the street and wiped his forehead with his arm. Aisha passed Nivritti five US dollars.

"No, this is too much!" Nivritti told her.

Aisha narrowed her eyes at Nivritti and removed two of the one-dollar bills from her hand. "Give this to him then," Aisha instructed her.

Nivritti reluctantly handed the human rickshaw worker three US dollars. He smiled, showing a few teeth in his mouth, and bowed with folded hands to both women before singing a Hindi song while navigating down Ganesh Chandra Avenue with his rickshaw.

Nivritti smirked and turned toward Aisha. "Told you," she said, shrugging her shoulders.

Aisha shook her head. "So where should we meet tomorrow?" she asked, beginning to walk up the steps to the Broadway Hotel.

"It's time that I show you the district. Take the prepaid taxi to Sonagachi. They will know how to get you there, and most taxi drivers know a little English, so you should be OK with translation. If not, ask a concierge to help you. Be in modest sari attire tomorrow. Cover your necklace up." Nivritti walked up to the same step Aisha was on and placed Aisha's necklace inside her sari. "See? Hide it like this. Do not bring a camera with you. I recommend taking a pad and pen with you, though, and hide those somewhere on you. If you have a small change purse with you, take that instead of a noticeable pocketbook. Make sure the taxi lets you off on Chittaranjan Avenue. The cost should be no more than 140 rupees to get you there. Let's meet around noon." Nivritti pulled out her cell phone. "I'm calling my husband to see where he and I are going to meet for dinner. Get some more sleep, Shadow; you're going to need it for tomorrow."

The Red-Light District
वेश्यावृर्त प्रभावति जलिा

Aisha arrived in the northern part of Kolkata known as Sonagachi. She used a prepaid taxi that made her pay 150 rupees. The night before, she read through her binder that the *Hartford Journal* provided her and noticed that most transportation could be negotiated, rather than a fixed price. So she reluctantly paid for the fare, as that would be expensed through her company anyway. On her ride over, she passed a beautiful palace that looked to be built many years ago but well preserved. She found out from the taxi driver, who spoke some English, that it had been built by a wealthy Bengali merchant whose descendants still inhabited the marble-walled manor. The home had been filled with classical Western and Eastern artwork since the nineteenth century. She passed by the mansion and its pristine neighborhood, and no less than ten minutes after, she came into an area that had litter scattered on every street and around outdoor bazaars. *Contradictive India*, Aisha thought to herself.

After getting out of the taxi, Aisha saw Nivritti engrossed in a passionate conversation with another woman in a sari that looked disheveled and unclean on some parts. She walked up to the two women, and the one woman stopped engaging in the discussion with Nivritti and looked Aisha up and down.

"*O Mere Bhagwan!*" The woman's eyes widened.

Nivritti stopped talking and noticed the woman's glance toward Aisha. Aisha stared back at the women, her eyes darting between the two of them. Nivritti said something in Hindi to the woman again, and the female crossed her arms in front of her chest.

Nivritti grabbed Aisha and pulled her a couple of paces away from the woman, toward a small clothing bazaar. "Listen, Shadow, I can't go all the way in with you. That is Charita. She told me I can walk you only as far as she allows me to, and then I'll have to walk back up here to wait for you, if I should choose to," Nivritti explained.

Aisha suddenly got nervous, not knowing why the woman did not want Nivritti to accompany them. She thought of her family and of course Majid and the concerns he shared with her before she left. "I will only go where you go then; I have to protect myself," Aisha explained with a worried look on her face.

Nivritti shook her head quickly. "No, Shadow, you must complete the assignment; they will not hurt you, especially after the way she looked at you. You will not be harmed by anyone there. Besides, you're already protected." Nivritti touched Aisha's collar bone. "If you're going to marry an Indian man, you have to believe in our customs, have faith in them. Now go." Nivritti took Aisha by the shoulders and pushed her toward Charita.

Charita smiled at Aisha and curtsied slightly to her and walked them through the main area of the district. There were many people in the area, and it was difficult to walk through. There was litter everywhere, and Aisha looked through small pockets of alleyways in between buildings and saw silhouettes of people. She noticed a little girl sobbing to herself on the street, rocking herself back and forth with her knees to her chest. Other people around them did not seem to notice and were walking into the little girl. She was shoved around slightly by the people walking by. Aisha stopped walking and left Nivritti and Charita to backtrack to the little girl. Aisha slowly sauntered back over to the little girl sobbing and bent down to touch her shoulder. The girl looked frightened and backed away from Aisha. Aisha felt confused by the little girl's behavior, seeing that she had come to comfort her. She removed from her change purse two US dollars and placed the money in the girl's hands. The girl immediately stopped crying, smirked in Aisha's face, got up, and ran into a dark alley.

Aisha stood up, looking confused. She took out her cell phone to call Nivritti, and suddenly someone snatched the phone from her. "What the hell!" Aisha looked at the guy who confiscated her phone.

He said something in Hindi and walked away from her. Aisha grabbed her head and was in total shock. She began to follow the man in the alley, yelling, "He's got my phone! Someone stop him!"

She made sure she kept her eyes fixed on the bloodred-colored shirt he had on. It stood out among the crowd of mostly earth tones. She saw the guy run into a narrow doorway, and she ran through it, a few moments behind him. When she got in the building, she saw the same girl who had been weeping. The little girl's eyes were dried from crying. The girl handed an older woman the money. The older woman placed the money inside her sari, between her breasts.

Damn it! You just got hustled! Aisha thought to herself, shaking her head. "Some guy ran into here, and he has my cell phone," Aisha said in slow English, trying her best to remain calm.

The woman narrowed her eyes at Aisha and looked her up and down with disdain. The woman pushed Aisha's right shoulder and continued to shove her out of the building and slammed the door in her face. Aisha fell, almost landing on someone's feet. She looked up and noticed Nivritti standing above her.

Nivritti held her hand out for Aisha to grab. "You were supposed to stay close to us!" Nivritti scolded Aisha.

Aisha used Nivritti's help to get off the ground and brushed the dirt off her sari. "I know. Some guy took my cell phone. He's in this building behind me." Aisha pointed.

"Come. Stay beside me and don't say a word."

Nivritti opened the door and held out her badge that showed she was from the consulate. She yelled at the woman who just pushed Aisha out of the building and shoved the badge in her face. Nivritti spoke in Hindi to the woman, who gave her some back talk until she finally called the guy over who had taken Aisha's phone. The guy came out of the shadows and reluctantly held out his hand for Aisha to grab the cell phone. Aisha snatched the phone from his hand, and she and Nivritti left the building.

"Thanks, Nivritti. Look, this happened because I happened to notice a little girl sobbing on the street, and I felt bad for her, so I gave her some cash," Aisha explained as they caught up to Charita.

"Don't ever provide money here to anyone, including street children, who know how to play you for a sucker," Nivritti said.

Aisha, for the first time in speaking with Nivritti, did not have a clever rebuttal but just grew silent and kept on walking down the street with her. They reached a high-rise building, and Charita stopped in front of it and turned to face the women. She spoke to Nivritti in Hindi and went inside of the building.

Aisha was about to walk in as well, until she noticed Nivritti waiting outside. "Aren't you coming?" she asked her.

"No. This is as far as she told me I can go. The rest of the journey is yours to take—alone. Listen, there are some consulate undercover guards walking around here; I've seen a few. You are protected, Shadow, physically and spiritually. Go; remember to write down your journey when you get back to your hotel. Keep your belongings on you at all times, and text me after you leave here every day."

Nivritti was about to walk away, when Aisha grabbed her arm. "You're not going to stay or at least hang out closer to the bazaars on Chittaranjan Avenue?" Aisha asked, hoping she would say yes.

"No. Text me when you get back to the hotel." Nivritti turned away and disappeared through the crowd.

Aisha laughed, throwing her head up to the sky, and walked in the building. She heard music that she assumed was being sung in Hindi; the lyrics had a Tantric, sultry sound. She saw young women being taught how to belly dance.

Charita was waiting a ways away from the entranceway for Aisha. "Come." She gestured her hand to Aisha to follow her.

They passed one of the young women who was being taught by an older woman how to dance. When it appeared she got a move wrong, the older woman smacked her back and did it so forcefully that she fell to the ground. Aisha was stunned and looked at Charita, who shook her head at Aisha. She took it as a warning to not get involved and to keep walking. Charita greeted people in Hindi as they walked by them, and they entered another room filled with smoke and sculptured deities. Charita got on her knees and prayed in front of an idol of a goddess who had a dark blue complexion and four arms and sat on a lotus flower with four elephants around her. Aisha looked at the statue.

"This is Kamala. She is Lakshmi's incarnation. Goddess of wisdom. To receive her gifts, you must wear something close to your heart," Charita said.

"You speak English, I see," Aisha said, respecting the statue in Charita's presence and bowing subtly to it.

"Yes, I do. What I have to share with you is really only for you to know, not your interpreter. You have a big heart, just like

Lakshmi…I mean, you know her as Black Gold. During her time, though, things were a bit different. People could be taken as genuine; things are different now. Your giving nature could get the best of you out here. Look to your guides to help you figure out someone's true nature," Charita advised.

"What guides? My guide was supposed to be Nivritti," Aisha said, getting agitated by Charita's ambiguous talk.

"Nivritti works for the consulate and does not possess the spirit you do. She served her purpose; the gods never lie. Her presumptuous nature blinds her from seeing truth; she got as far as her comprehension will allow her to. The filth, the deceitful people—she saw what her spirit allowed her to see, nothing more and nothing less. You will see more, much more, because your heart is pure. You can see rubbish all around you but believe something beautiful grows underneath it. That's why you can go farther," Charita explained.

These people have a clever way with words, Aisha thought. "OK…So can I meet her?" Aisha asked, rubbing her hands together. Charita looked confused. "The boss chick," Aisha said. "You know: the one who looks like me, got it goin' on obviously, since you treat her like a god…Black Gold!" she spat out excitedly.

Charita smirked. "So you think she was a prostitute and that is why she was called Black Gold, huh?" Charita crossed her arms.

"Well, yeah," Aisha said in an annoyed fashion.

"Boy, do you have a lot to learn. From an enchanted perspective, gold is pure, holy, and should not be exploited. You're not ready to meet her. She will probably not see you yet…if ever."

Charita began to walk down the hallway with Aisha directly behind her. She opened a back door for them to go outside again. She greeted another woman and picked up two plates. "Here, it's time for us to eat." Charita handed the plate to Aisha.

Aisha's eyes got wide. *Oh, damn! I don't know what they're about to feed me. I pray I don't get sick, but I'd better eat some of this food so I can gain at least a fraction of their trust,* she thought to herself.

Aisha got in line behind Charita, who was talking, gesturing with her hands to some of the women in the brothel. Aisha noticed how Charita was speaking in an aggressive manner toward the women, as they were with her. A little girl pushed Aisha out of the way to get to a pot filled with a stew. Aisha was about to cuss the girl out but humbled herself and allowed the girl to get in front of her.

Charita had seen what happened. "This might be Leela's first meal for today. She is a playful little thing; don't be upset," Charita said, pouring the stew on Aisha's plate. Charita yelled back at the girl in Hindi.

Leela looked back and stuck her tongue out and continued to run away, holding her plate of food.

Aisha ate lunch with Charita's mother, sisters, and a few cousins in the brothel, where they all stayed. None of the other women spoke fluent English, and it was a rather peculiar thing to Aisha. The women had Charita translate funny stories to Aisha, who saw the humor in them and gained a respect for them.

How can they be in such a situation like this but maintain such resilient spirits? she thought to herself.

Just as one of Charita's sisters was about to share another story, a man walked up to their circle. He had a bottle in his hand, took a swig of it, and smashed it on the building opposite of theirs. He got in Charita's sister's face, spewing Hindi words at her. Charita's sister kept looking down and pushed her plate toward her cousin. Her mouth was quivering as she got up and allowed the man to take her by the hand. Aisha's eyes were wide, and the other women began to laugh.

Confused, Aisha asked Charita, "What the hell just happened?"

Charita stopped laughing to explain. "We laugh to keep from crying. He is one of her regulars. He's actually an OK guy. We think it's like foreplay to him. He gifts her very well, never puts marks on her body, and is willing to use a condom too. Tarala is lucky. We all wish we had a giving one like that. He is never rough with her, treats her so nice; she even receives pleasure from him too. Most of our guys are mean and nasty; we rarely enjoy it." Charita was about to continue, when she heard a faint bell ring. "She is here. We must go back. Come with me!"

Charita pushed their plates back to her cousin, who was beginning to wash their dishes in a bowl filled with water and suds. She grabbed Aisha's arm forcefully as they ran to the other building. They ran from room to room until they arrived back at the deity shrines.

Charita let go of Aisha's arm and looked around rapidly. "Where is she? That was her call to let us know she is here." The corners of Charita's mouth were tight until she saw a bunch of papers underneath the goddess Kamala.

The papers were khaki colored, very old fashioned in appearance. The script was in English but written in calligraphy with a felt pen. The words written on the letter began with: *For Shadow*. Charita immediately handed Aisha the papers. They were taped together. Aisha ripped a crease to open it and was about to recite to Charita what was written.

"Stop!" Charita placed her hands up to her ears to cover them. "You must not. It says for you only." She pushed Aisha toward the front entrance of the building and began to walk with her until they got back to the beginning of Chittaranjan Avenue near a bazaar. "I'll see you tomorrow, Shadow, at eleven a.m.. My family and I...We like you a lot," Charita confessed with a smile before walking back to the brothel.

These people are going to stop pushing me, Aisha thought, fixing her sari. She hailed a taxi and instructed the driver to take her to the Broadway Hotel on Ganesh Chandra Avenue.

☾

Aisha got to her hotel room around 5:00 p.m. and removed her sari that was soiled from her sitting on the street in the brothel with the women. She placed the sari in a laundry bag and hung it on her door for housekeeping to take to clean for her. She took a shower and washed her hair. She placed her robe on afterward and text messaged Nivritti that she was back in her hotel room—safe. She watched some TV and fell asleep during a show. When she woke up, it was 10:00 p.m.

She looked at her phone and saw that Majid had text messaged her:

> I had the filthiest fantasy of you and me; I wish you picked up the phone. Professor Khan needs you to call him back ASAP!

"How is he going to get through the next eighty-eight days?" she said.

She realized it was around 12:30 p.m. in the United States and figured Majid was in class. She text messaged him instead:

> My bad, babe. I was meeting people for the assignment. I am safe. Do not worry. Can't wait to hear Professor Khan's filthy lecture. When you can't reach me by voice, text me all your dirty thoughts... xoxo.

She smiled as she sent the message to Majid and turned to her nightstand. She read the calligraphy again: *For Shadow*. She grew intrigued by the papers and unfolded them. She noticed there were three pages. The right edges of the papers were feathered as if they had been torn from a journal. She shuffled through the papers to notice that each one had a date. She turned on the lamp on her nightstand and began to read.

LOST JOURNALS
गुम हो चुकी पत्रिकाएँ

10/10/1993

I arrived in Kolkata bright and early this morning. The people were not too friendly. They looked at me a couple of times and then turned away when I asked them for directions. This city is not the friendliest when it comes to navigation. The airport needs to be remodeled. I saw all kinds of strange and unusual things that made me cringe. This is home...for now; better get used to it. Of course the Evening Star let the black person go on assignment without providing a date the assignment is to be completed nor a plane ticket for when I'd return to the States—some sacrificial lamb I've become.

It's just as well...I have nothing to go back to. No eligible bachelors in the US, just the same ole fellas. I've always been the outlier in the family. Moving from Mississippi to Connecticut was as adventurous as my parents were ever going to get. When my brother wanted something, he got it from me. I would do anything for him, including place his needs before mine—always. Being the oldest of the two of us was rough on me. I always had a curiosity for the mysteries of life. When everyone saw just what lay on the surface, I had the talent to see underneath. This made me very unusual, and my family knew that.

I, at times, have caught my mother looking at me in the most peculiar way. Makes me remember the moments she would often tell my elementary school teachers and baby-sitters, This is not my child. I don't know whose child this is. This comment was usually followed by a gut-busting southern laugh. Black people love to laugh at everything—especially their pain. I never developed that habit because I knew I'd always have to come back to my pain, so I'd prefer to figure out what the cause was rather than continuously medicate it. Laughter eventually goes away, but the pain never does until you deal with it. That's me. I'm always thinking into things. Seeing the unseen, discovering what lies beneath.

Although Dad never got me, he accepted me as his child and my many unique behaviors. Before I left on assignment, I remember my parents looking confused, as if I had just said I was going to Mars and wasn't sure when I would get back. The good-bye between my family and I was rather quick and to the point. This seems strange to write, but I feel like I reached a crossroads and that my journey with my family ended the day I got on the airplane.

I've always been in search of something. I can only describe it as a feeling; not quite sure what it is, but when I find it, I'll know it was what I was missing. I can only identify this feeling as a quest for understanding and wholeness. I sometimes feel lost, not sure which road to take, and this feeling bothers me. When you're not sure of your path, there will always be someone around to lead you down there, and it might not be the right one for you.

Ugh! My taxi just pulled up. I pray the driver knows English. I'm not expecting the Four Seasons once I get to my destination, as if the plane ride was not nerve-racking enough... Let's see where Kolkata takes me.

10/15/1993

Boy, oh boy, what a difference five days makes. My assignment concerns me—my boss and his unclear instructions. I felt some kind of way about how he views this country and the people. His instructions were to find out how Kolkata was becoming a fast-growing metropolis. What was their secret—was it their deities or British influence? This assignment could take forever. Number one, I do not speak their language, so that presents the biggest barrier. And number two, where do you begin in understanding a country you've never lived in? As my boss said to me before I left, "You're a great journalist, Jenkins. Write us something spectacular!"

In my growing frustration, I began to write a couple of pages in my nook of a room, but then something happened to me. I looked at my computer screen and completely erased everything I wrote. I do not know what came over me. I couldn't stomach what was written. It was too collegiate, too made up, too synthetic. The Evening Star wouldn't know the difference though, right? But I would, and that's what irritated me.

I left my room. It was so damn small, and I felt like I was being suffocated inside of it. I decided to walk the streets and did so for hours. To understand a city like this, you must be of it; I at least understood that much.

I stopped in a marketplace for some Bengali food, when a mass of people ran to a brand new '93 Black Mercedes-Benz with gold rims. "Vishnu!" That's all I heard a passerby say.

As I was about to enjoy my last morsel of a grilled shrimp dish cooked in a flavored coconut-based curry sauce, some idiot pushed into me to get to the car of an apparently famous celebrity of Kolkata. He knocked the last bite of my seafood dish off of my plate. I groaned in annoyance at this but then figured I'd look at the person who had everyone in town so enthralled. I joined the crowd and waited to see who they were in awe of. The passenger window rolled down to reveal a pair of brown eyes and thick black eyebrows. He held his hand out of the window, waving at the people. Some children asked him for money, men spoke blessings to him, and women gave him flirtatious stares. I was only a few paces away and looked at him in an annoyed manner since this was the person that ruined my meal.

As his car rode slowly through the crowd, I walked along, continuing to look at the powerful man. He was not a bad-looking man—in fact, one of the best-looking men I've ever seen. Among the smiles and admiration, he noticed me. I grimaced and had an accusing facial expression. We had a staring match for a few moments. It was as if he was waiting for my face to soften. Seeing a man that fine, I could not help but soften my features to his stare. After all, once we matched stares, everyone in the vicinity disappeared and no longer mattered.

As a smile spread across my face, he looked down at my attire and began to point and laugh. "You're a messy little thing. In India we make sure our food ends up in our mouths, not on our clothes! Ha-ha!"

I was mortified and couldn't help but look down. I had on a beautiful white sari that was ruined by the passerby who made the coconut curried sauce hit my clothing. My smile turned into a grimace, and I threw my plastic fork at his car and crossed my arms. I stopped walking as his car rode down the street. He looked back once and blew me a kiss and rolled up his window. The car he was in picked up speed to lose the people and turned onto the next street.

 I didn't know what to think; I was flabbergasted. Was that kiss directed at me? It couldn't have been. I picked up a napkin and tried to remove the stain, but all it did was continue to smear into my white shirt. Feeling like a slob after meeting (my guess) a Bollywood actor, I felt embarrassed and hailed a taxi. The taxi approached a less scenic area, and to this day I do not know what made me get out of the taxi, but something did. I paid the fare and got out.

 I heard melodic music coming from an alleyway. Inside the alley I saw human beings in the worst conditions I've ever seen in my life. Now, my family grew up poor in Mississippi. For thirteen years we lived in a one-level, two-bedroom house with one bathroom for four people to share before moving up to Connecticut; conditions weren't much different there either. It never seemed like we had enough of anything. I remember my mother cutting coupons all the time before going food shopping. It was considered a treat for us kids when our parents could get more than just the bare minimum for the house on their minimum-wage paychecks. I never knew that it could be worse than that.

 On the street I passed silhouette figures of a man and woman engaged in oral sex. The woman had her skirt hiked up, and her knees were bare on the muddy dirt road. The man she was giving pleasure to grabbed her head and pulled it side to side as a child that looked the age of eight ran by them. I gasped, not understanding how they could conduct themselves in public like that. The sad part is that the male child made a gesture with his pants toward the woman. The older man shooed the child away from the scene. The little boy ran off into the night, holding an action figure toy in his hand, with no guardian around looking for him. I was thoroughly disgusted at this point. The man began to groan, and he pulled the woman's head as he said something to her. Although her back was to me, I could literally see her body rise up and down after swallowing his cum. I felt like throwing up. The man zipped up his pants and threw money at her before walking away. As he walked away, the mud from the streets hit her in the face. She used the money he threw at her to clear the mud from her face. This woman did not have any emotion to her. She looked indifferent, as if she already knew she was nothing—so it did not matter who did what to her. I wanted to cry for her. I'd never seen such a sight like this before.

I thought to keep walking, and then a man approached me. He grabbed me by the shoulders and said something in a language I did not understand. I hit a concrete wall. I was trying to get him off of me just as another Indian man approached us. He grabbed the guy who attacked me and spoke to him in a surprisingly calm manner. The first guy looked shocked after the man was done talking to him, and he ran away. My hero's name was Dr. Jana, and at that moment, my purpose for being in Kolkata was found.

☾

Aisha placed the papers down on the nightstand; she felt exhausted. *Oh my God*, she thought. *I can't believe that happened. How would I react if I saw something like that?*

Feeling like she had read enough for the evening, she cradled herself in the fetal position and looked at her phone. She noticed she had three text messages from Majid. "Not tonight, babe," she said somberly to herself. She sent a "Good night" text message to him without looking at his response, and she fell asleep.

Who Do You Think You Are? A Hero?
खुद को क्या समझते हैं? एक नायक?

Aisha woke at 6:00 a.m. Her body felt drained, especially her legs from all of the walking she did the day before. She took a shower, brushed her teeth, and dialed room service. Her thoughts roamed to the journal pages. Having woken up so early, she had time to read a couple more entries before taking a taxi over to Chittaranjan Avenue. She felt bad for dismissing quality time with Majid, but her heart had grown heavy after reading the last entry. She was in no mood to entertain his pleasures the way he deserved. She heard a knock on her hotel room door and discovered it was her breakfast. She had the waiter place the items on the desk in the room. She began to dig into her food and read the next entry from Cyndi Jenkins.

10/20/1993

Dr. Jana taught me the ins and outs of Kolkata: things that only a person who grew up here knows. I received a wealth of information from him; I figured I'd have my story in no time to provide to the Evening Star. I knew I had to be humble and not rush him by aggressively asking about the business world of Kolkata. He knew lots of people in the business district, as some of his relatives worked in financial services, but I noticed very quickly what a lot of other foreign journalists may not have noticed. Money does not drive these people. You meet a culture of people and instantly know if all they care about is money and control, not them—no.

I would start my day people watching. For instance, I've taken notice of the beautiful Mulik Ghat Flower Market. It fascinates me to see businessmen leave the commerce district, walk into the rural area of the flower market to purchase flowers for their homes, and stop in to pray at one of the oldest Hindu Temples in Kolkata—Khalighat Kali Temple—before finally going home to their families. Indians—well, the majority of them—have traditional values. I grew warmly accustomed to seeing at 6:00 p.m., on the dot, an Indian businessman come home to accompany his wife and newborn baby on a stroll through Sudder Street. He never missed a day. While he was at work, I'd see his wife going to the market or placing clothes on their outside clothesline.

West Bengal people have traditional values and seem to stick to them, while at the same time their people are becoming more educated and their businesses are budding. The world is looking to find India's secret. Indians seem indifferent to the spotlight the world places on them as they continue to grow economically, which means materially, but steadily preserving their culture. This is not to say this won't change, as I see the younger generations wearing jeans and speaking back to their parents, but it does not look to be changing on a mass level in the near future.

I was learning all of India's culture from Dr. Jana, until one day he finally allowed me to work with him for his center. I would go from brothel to brothel, speaking to the women on the importance of contraceptives and also promoting the other nongovernment-funded groups who were there to provide free clinical checkups. My assignment with the paper began to become less of a priority now that I had found a story worth experiencing and sharing.

I took a break one day from speaking and entered a makeshift pub not too far from Chittaranjan Avenue. I plopped down on a stool and asked for a cold glass of bangla. I sat next to a man smoking a cigar, and he rudely exhaled the smoke in my direction. I moved chairs so I wouldn't have to sit directly next to him, and he did it again.

"Excuse you!" I said to the man, waving the smoke from my face.

"I thought that would get your attention," he said with a Indian accent mixed with a hint of an English accent. "I've been told in some cultures that when a man blows smoke in a woman's direction, it means he's got an eye for her," he said, changing stools to sit right beside me again.

I looked over, and it was the man from the Mercedes-Benz, who the people referred to as Vishnu. He was alone this time, in the finest of clothing I've ever seen someone in the district wear, and he was still appealing. I looked down to make sure there were no food stains to tease and taunt me with, and then I looked back up, noticing all was good.

"Thanks," I said to the bartender as he passed me my drink.

"You know, kitten, I prefer wine. It is a much classier beverage, especially for an American girl like yourself. She'll have some tadi next," he instructed the bartender. I looked at him, annoyed. "You'll like it. It's similar in appearance to a cream-based liquor, but it's created from the sap of date palms and coconut palms, sweet and succulent. You must try."

The bartender poured the drink for me in a wine-shaped glass with gold trimming and left it for me on the bar. I did not want to rub anyone the wrong way here, and seeing that he was like a boss around Kolkata, I complied. When I tasted the drink, it was absolutely decadent and filling. He noticed my positive reaction and experienced pleasure from it.

Our moment was stopped abruptly when a scared woman ran into the pub with her clothes tattered. She spoke in Hindi to the bartender. I could not make out the conversation, but his hand gestures explained to me that he wanted her to leave the pub immediately. She left reluctantly. I watched in horror as a man walked up to her and slapped the daylights out of her face. She fell to the ground and spit out blood. My new purpose gave me strength to want to save this woman.

As I was getting up to leave to take care of the situation, Vishnu grabbed my hand and set me back down. His stare was stern. "So you save people. That's what you're doing in Kolkata is saving people. You don't know what you are getting yourself into, kitten. You're in Sonagachi. What do you expect? If you had a man in your life, perhaps you wouldn't look like you're always hissing at men! Ha-ha!" Vishnu had the same snarly laugh as the first day I met him.

"I volunteer for an organization that can help her, she doesn't have to take this abuse." With that, I tried to get up again and leave.

He took me by the hand and this time did it more forcefully. We looked out of the pub again, and the two people once engaged in a physical assault were now gone from our view.

Vishnu gently grabbed my chin to face him. "Like I said, you do not know what you're getting yourself into. Who do you think you are? A hero? That's what you do: save people. You can't even save yourself. What makes you think you'll save another fresh piece of tail? You don't think you're being followed? I see you. You go to a hotel on Sudder Street every night. You don't live like these girls. How can you help someone you don't understand? You must think you're British. Let me guess: you consider yourself a missionary, and you call our deities false idols. You're nothing but these girls' false idol. You spend a couple of hours here and then go back to your plush bed on Sudder Street, dreaming about me. You're not a hero, kitten," Vishnu concluded.

I was rather put off about the second-to-last comment he made but thought it better to stick to the main subject of our debate. "And you are? I've learned a thing or two about your gods—why do your people call you Vishnu? What have you done that is so extraordinary?" I asked, knowing that I was pressing my luck with a boss such as himself.

He looked at me in a defiant manner and put his cigar down. "I provide balance. This place is not a moral quagmire for me. Some of these women—well, let me put it this way: this is all some of them know. You want to take them out of this place and do what with them? Some of these women had a choice to move on but decided to come back here. Take her for instance."

He pointed to a woman standing on the corner whose brown complexion had reddish undertones. She had on a cream-colored head scarf and placed her hands on her hips. She called a man over to her and began to speak sweet nothings in his ear. The guy looked to be a businessman, quite possibly from Sudder Street's business district. As she was speaking, he closed his eyes, licking his lips. She skillfully removed his wallet from his trousers.

"That's Elina. Let me tell you...She's good." Vishnu continued his story, making a satisfied hand gesture. "The best head I ever received in West Bengal! She speaks fluent English and French. Very smart girl. A couple of European volunteers who have organizations here tried to coerce her to leave as well. She went on a program to study in France for some time but came back. Her mother, father, and brother are here. She is so gifted at what she does. When she left, her family needed money. Her father is strung out on drugs, her mother is sick, and her brother is physically disabled, not capable of finding work to make ends meet. So who's going to take care of her family? The European missionaries promised her riches, but their riches take time to attain. When you have a tragic story like hers, time is not on your side. So, hero, what should she do?" Vishnu said, looking me up and down, inhaling his cigar.

My mind began to think on a whole different level. I could not answer his question! I wanted to answer it, but my answer would not make sense. At the same time, I could not help but be attracted to his street bravado and brazenness—I had to leave. He figured me out. I was exposed, caught red-handed, and it did not take long at all for him to do. He waited patiently for my answers. I looked him in his eyes—what a big mistake—I still think, even now, that is what captured me. I realized there was nowhere to run and began to like the thrill of being exposed—of course by him only.

"To dignify your question with an answer: psychologists have researched the complexities of human behavior for years, and in order for people to change their situations, they have to learn how to get comfortable with being uncomfortable. It sounds easy, but it's not. Leaving everything you know and having the patience and perseverance to work toward making a better life is easier said than can be done sometimes. I have to get back to Chittaranjan Avenue—I am tutoring one of the girls," I finished responding to him, getting up from the stool.

"How delightful," he said coldly. "What subject are you teaching her, kitten?" he asked me, placing the cigar back in his mouth.

I turned around, getting terribly irritated by his demeaning nickname for me. "My goal is to get her up to speed in her age group, starting first with learning English. We are reading Shakespeare's Romeo and Juliet—you wouldn't know anything about that though." Yes! I finally had a witty comeback for the handsome brute. I began to proudly walk away, when I heard his stool turn in my direction.

"'What's in a name that which we call a rose, by any other word would smell as sweet'...said by Juliet."

I thought my ears had deceived me. I turned around, perplexed and intrigued at the same time. "I have to get back," I said again, feeling defeated by the charms of this man.

"Why go so soon? We're just getting to know each other." He placed his cigar down in the ashtray, got up, and held both of my hands; we faced each other. I noticed how much taller he was than me. My biggest weakness in the world is a man—and a gorgeous one at that!

Don't look in his eyes—anywhere but his eyes, I said to myself.

"I volunteer for a small research group; they are expecting me back soon. I must go," I said, trying to break away from his grasp...Well, not really.

"I know you do. The health scientist is from Kolkata. He gets these people because these are his people—like me. I finance his program; just tell them you're with me."

He stepped closer to me, and I could feel his lips on my forehead. My body began to twitch. What the hell? That's never happened before...with my clothes still on and no "work" involved.

"Please...I must go. Thanks for the drinks," I said weakly.

"Do you know why you've been kept safe for so long on the streets fighting crime, kitten?"

Damn it! How does he know how to keep my interest? I thought.

"No! I don't know," I expressed, my knees feeling unsteady.

"I told every 'john' out there that you're mine, and if they were to lay a hand on you, I'd remove their intestines from their bodies and sell their organs on the black market. Your cute little hero hat and sassy attitude don't mean a thing here." He smirked, let go of my hands, and walked back to his cigar.

I grew annoyed again at him sizing me up and telling me that my efforts were in vain. "My name is not kitten, jerk off," I mumbled as I began to leave.

"I know that, Cyndi. We'll see each other again. Try not to miss me too much. Good luck on your endeavors. After all, you know the saying: a little goes...well...a little way." He laughed at his comment and walked inside another room of the pub.

I left feeling vulnerable and exposed. He might as well have beaten me until my body turned red, strip me naked, and had me walk the streets bare. I admitted to myself once I got back to familiar people and territory that I was dangerously attracted to the man who explained his profession as providing balance to Sonagachi and who fashioned himself in so many words to be my protector.

I thought Majid had the moves. No wonder she's falling for him, Aisha thought. She wiped her mouth with a napkin and placed her breakfast tray outside of her hotel door. She opened the curtains and peered outside. It was a sunny day, and temperature-wise it felt like close to eighty. She noticed traffic was congested on the streets and looked at the clock in her room, which read 9:30 a.m. She turned on the little TV and got somewhat bored due to the language barrier. She decided to call Majid to see if he was awake.

When she called, he immediately answered on the first ring. "How's my naughty girl?"

Aisha rolled her eyes. *Men really do have a one-track mind,* she thought. "I'm doing well, sweetie. Phone sex is going to be a little difficult, boo. See, we are in different sceneries, which can make it difficult to set the mood at times," Aisha said, sitting on the bed.

"What do you mean, Isha?" he asked, perplexed.

"Sweetheart, where I am, it's bright, sunny—" She stopped short as he finished the answer.

"And where I am, it's midnight and quiet. I gotcha, Isha, but a little change in scenery can be done on your part—if you're up to it," Majid concluded.

Aisha smiled, as she never liked to leave her dude hanging. She turned off the TV, closed the drapes, and placed the Do Not Disturb sign on the hotel room door. She lay on the bed and switched her phone to speaker. "I'm ready for my lecture, the subject being dirty fantasies, starring Professor Khan and Aisha Benson..."

This Is Our Life
यह हमारा जीवन है

Aisha returned to Chittaranjan Avenue and walked by herself over to the building with the goddess Kamala. She went inside and saw a few teenage girls praying. One had on a yellow *choli,* with a matching skirt and a nose ring necklace that connected to her right ear. She had red dye in between her eyebrows. Her friend had on a red *choli,* with the same red dye in between her eyebrows. They both wore tattered flip-flops. When they saw Aisha, they stood up.

"It's OK; no worries. Please continue."

Aisha was walking to the back door exit, when an old, heavyset woman walked over to the girls and said something in Hindi to the both of them. She slapped their hands and pushed their shoulders around slightly. The girls kept their heads down and shoulders slouched as the woman continued to berate them. After the woman was done, she and the two girls walked to the exit, where two men were waiting. These men were dressed in regular, casual clothing. The older woman pushed a girl to each man. The girls reluctantly pulled the men by the arm to adjacent doorways before closing them.

From reading Cyndi's journal entries, Aisha knew better than to get involved. *Although it's nothing like seeing it for yourself; you never know how you would react to such a sight*, Aisha thought.

"Girls make money; never-touched girls make more money!" the woman yelled at Aisha and then walked away to clean some clothes.

Aisha shook her head in amazement and continued down the alleyway, trying to remember where Charita and her family ate lunch. Once she found the area, she bent down to sit on a plastic crate and decided to just wait until she saw Charita walk by.

Thirty minutes passed and Charita busted through a doorway with a man behind her. They were both laughing hysterically. She was holding his hand, but just as he noticed Aisha looking over to them, he threw her hand away and took out his wallet. He slurred something in Hindi to Charita and shoved her, and the force knocked her to the ground. The man hurled money at her. Aisha could not make out if she was still laughing or sobbing, as they were a couple of feet away from her. From behind him, Charita grabbed onto the man's leg, and he wiggled out of her grasp before walking briskly by Aisha, nudging her on the right shoulder. She ignored the man, acknowledging Charita had the worse of the two situations. Charita crawled over to the side of the building and sat there. Aisha picked up the money for her and bent down to hand it to her.

"No! He shouldn't have done that to me! It's because you saw us...holding hands. He's embarrassed of me!" She began to cry.

Aisha focused her eyes on Charita. "Why do you do this to yourself? You seem like one of the women who could fare so much better," Aisha said, now placing her arm around Charita's shoulders.

"Yeah, right this is our life. With all of this encouragement, perhaps you should have been my mother, or rather Lakshmi should have been. She tried to help. I was supposed to be one of the ones..." Charita trailed off and put her head down on her lap.

Aisha did not want to probe. She took the money the john threw, rolled it up, and placed it in Charita's hand.

"I felt it. For one moment I felt what it was like." Charita looked up to Aisha. Her eyes were watery and red from the combination of crying and being drunk.

"What was it? What did you feel?" Aisha asked with genuine empathy for Charita's situation.

"I felt the purity, honesty, and acceptance. He had me feel it. I felt lucky. I felt love. Even though it was in passing, he made me feel it." She smiled meekly and then turned her head down.

Aisha shook her head and watched a tear fall from her own eye. "Charita, don't ever see him again! If he's playing with your mind, it's not healthy for you." That was all Aisha could think to say to her at that moment.

"Yeah, sure—me empower myself after all of these years. Look around you. What is exactly healthy? Aisha, that's your personality, not mine. He was embarrassed to be seen with a prostitute, that's all—nothing more and nothing less. In that moment he gave me...For the first time I felt like a princess. I plan on replaying that moment for as long as I live. The moment was so amazing that if I should never get it again, I feel I should be envied by every prostitute in the district. He gave me something to believe in; not many of us get that."

Charita stumbled around and, seeing her in such shape, Aisha helped walk her to where her family stayed. As Aisha got to Charita's bed, she did her best to not express her distaste for their living conditions. There were four small cots in a room that was already filled with pots and pans. One of her sisters was lying down and turned in the other direction in her sleep as they came in. Aisha helped Charita lie on the cot.

Charita's eyes glazed over, and before she fell asleep, she repeated, "I felt it."

Aisha looked around the room and noticed all of the books Charita had underneath her bed that were spilling out onto the other side of the room. She saw just about every literary novel she ever had to read in high school in America, taking particular notice of some of her favorites: *Catcher in the Rye, Moby Dick,* and *To Kill a Mocking Bird*. Even though the room was a terrible sight, it began to look better with the horde of books. To not wake anyone up, she shifted through the books quietly until she came to Shakespeare's *Romeo and Juliet*. Her eyes widened. She opened the book, and while turning the pages, a note came out:

> Charita,
> The hopeless romantic that you are! After teaching you how to read English with your very first American book, I knew it belonged to you. Read this book with all of the dreams of the world at your feet.
> —Cyndi

So Charita was the girl Cyndi read Romeo and Juliet *to? Oh my God! That makes perfect sense. How else could she have gotten this collection of books?* Aisha thought.

"Hey, what you doing here?" Aisha heard a woman bark at her from the bedroom door.

"I helped Charita to the bed. She was very drunk," Aisha answered, noticing that the woman was Charita's mother. The woman looked confused and could not comprehend—Aisha realized that she probably said the words too fast. She mimicked drunken movements and tilted an imaginary bottle to her mouth.

Charita's mom eventually nodded her head, acknowledging that she understood. "Charita like that. She get like that after Kamboja." Charita's mother began to giggle. "She say she love him. He love her too, for the moment…and then it's over. She get like that after, and in couple of hours, she meet another man and she better. Kamboja make her sick, make her feel love. He make her sick. He pay well though." Her mother marched into the room, unintentionally hitting Aisha in the shoulder, to quickly retrieve the money from Charita's hand as she slept. Aisha opened her mouth in amazement.

Charita's mother shrugged her shoulders and slipped the money into her chest area. "He make her sick. Should not love, just do. Much easier that way." She grunted and turned around to leave.

All Aisha could do was breathe deeply. She placed Charita's blanket on top of her shoulders and left the room. As she was walking out, she heard the same faint bell ring that Charita explained to her was that of Black Gold. She walked back to the temple, and once again Black Gold was nowhere to be found. She looked underneath the goddess Kamala to see a stack of journal entries slightly thicker than what she had received yesterday. She decided to read a few entries while Charita slept off the alcohol.

"I plan on staying as the night grows near. Do not punk out," Aisha said aloud to herself. She tapped her ankle to see if *Sally* was still skillfully taped to her. She smiled when she felt her taser gun, then read the next entry.

10/22/1993

I took a day off from the district to see the town of Kolkata. How beautiful a fall day it was in India. I love seeing leaves fall as the wind takes them on a journey. I enjoyed sightseeing but got quite nostalgic venturing around Kolkata by my lonesome self. How nice it would be to see the sights with someone else! Let's figure out why I don't have any men... Hmm, I can be very demanding, at times moody, a little too reserved, and judgmental. Well, growing up, my biggest fear was that I would end up like everyone else, staying in the same hood, pregnant at fourteen, and feeling like life could never get any better. I do remember some great guys in my neighborhood, but I never gave them the time of day. I was too focused on getting out and thought anyone and everything were toxic.

What I did not realize then that I realize now is that there is no running to a safe place. Your fears always catch up to you no matter where you are or who you are with. The last time I saw my fascinating protector, he read me like a book. How vulnerable I felt. Come to think about it, Vishnu is no different in personality than the street guys in my old neighborhoods of Mississippi and Connecticut. Was it that easy? Could it be that everyone read me this way?

I feel so strangely comfortable with him. The more he figured me out, the more I felt an invisible string pulling me toward him. He knew he had me the moment we saw each other. Hearing these thoughts in my head, I yearned to break away from them. I went to a bazaar to purchase head scarves of various color palettes, when I felt someone's stare in my direction. I turned to my right, and a man was standing outside of the bazaar with his hands folded in front of him as if he was waiting for me to finish my transaction. I looked his way but thought it better to walk in the opposite direction.

As I was about to turn the corner, the guy said with a Bengali accent, "You've already been down that road. Don't you want to know where this one will take you?" He gestured toward the walkway he was standing on. I looked him up and down. He had on brown slacks, with unpolished black shoes that looked a bit worn. His black silk textured shirt was only buttoned up to his stomach, revealing his chest hair and silver necklace. He looked like a slick-talking guy who thought he had more going on for him than what he really did. I was not interested in entertaining men of his type, so I ignored him and kept walking.

"Cyndi, he always knows where you are. Either you're going to cooperate, or you will continually have to meet up with me. And, believe me, you're not my type either," the slick-talking guy said.

I turned around slowly and said, "Who always knows where I am?" My face was expressionless even though I already knew who he was talking about.

"Follow me," the man said.

I walked a couple of feet behind him and followed him into a chic restaurant on Royd Street, not too far from my hotel.

We walked in and he greeted the host at the door. "She was sent for," said the slick-talking man.

I walked closer behind him into another room. The room had a small table in it, and seated at the table were Vishnu and another man. When they both saw me, Vishnu said something in Hindi to the other man sitting across from him. As that man walked away from the table, he smiled at me and then left the room.

"Brother, the English missionaries are looking for your donation; you told them you would provide that by this week," the slick guy said to Vishnu.

Vishnu replied back to the man in Hindi. I tried to make out by facial expression what he possibly said, but they both kept straight faces. The man finally left after a few moments.

"Sit down," Vishnu said, more of a command than a request. I sat down and placed my retail bag on my lap. "Buy anything I would like to see you in?" Vishnu asked, looking down at the bag.

I clenched up, grabbing the plastic bag, and did not answer the question. "So you also provide donations to the European missionaries?" I asked him, changing the subject.

"I do. The Europeans have brought their textbooks and resources for the women. For the rare few, they have provided education programs to sent them to their schools—a few women have gone, but most come back home," Vishnu affirmed.

I always noticed how intently his eyes focused on me. They felt like pointed arrows piercing my soul. I felt the rapture of being in a thrilling and suspenseful love story of our making, but still only comfortable with conversation.

"I am the complete opposite of these women. Contrary to what you think of me, I did not grow up well-off. I lived in a poor community back home—we call them ghettos. I did everything I could to get out of it," I explained to him.

"So you turned your back on your people then. No wonder you don't have a man in your life," Vishnu said matter-of-factly.

"Whatever. Let's not assume anything about one another, we don't know each other," I said as calmly as I could, remembering I was not in familiar territory and that I should hold back my usual brazen attitude.

"Oh, I know you, kitten...I know exactly who you are," Vishnu said with a deep baritone voice.

My body began to twitch yet again. How in the hell is he doing this? I thought. We had a staring match for a while that he won hands down, as I would look around continuously, feeling again naked and exposed but still not wanting to get up and leave.

"Look, I called you in here to ask you something: What are you doing here, Cyndi? I know you're a journalist from the US, but what journalist hangs out in Sonagachi without even so much as a camera? You take time in teaching the women and children how to read and take care of themselves. Who are you working for, honestly? The consulate—are you one of their people?" Vishnu asked me.

I could tell he was asking me this frankly, so I thought about the answer before replying. "I am a journalist. You're right about that. My boss sent me here without me knowing when I would be sent back to the US. The Indian economy is growing, and back home they are intrigued to hear the story of how certain states in India are fast becoming Meccas of financial success. When I got here, the goal I had in mind was to find that story, but I realized there are many answers to such a complicated question, and I no longer cared. I feel I have a bigger purpose to fulfill." I stopped talking to see if Vishnu was listening, and he was looking at me so attentively. I giggled slightly out of nervousness and continued. "When I met Dr. Jana, I found a bigger purpose than working for a paper back home on a story that has many answers. I believe these women are helping me just as much as I am helping them. I am beginning to find myself. I genuinely care for them and want to help them," I concluded.

Vishnu turned his head in the direction of a waiter that came in the room to provide us both drinks. "I'd like to make a toast." Vishnu put his glass in the air and gestured with his free hand for me to raise my glass as well. "To you, Cyndi. Your heart seems...genuine—I suppose."

We clinked glasses. I sipped the drink, noticing it was the tadi I had a couple of nights before. Since I loved it so much, I gulped down several sips until the glass was almost empty. I sat back in my chair, and after a minute or two, I felt lightheaded. I saw Vishnu watch me going into various states of intoxication. I felt incredibly confused and felt like the room was spinning.

"Now let me ask you again, Cyndi. Are you truly here out of the goodness of your heart, or do you also work for someone else with other intentions in mind?" Vishnu asked as he got up to assist me before I fell out of my chair. He sat me up, only to sit on the chair and place me in his lap.

"I love these girls, their families—I have no one to go back home to...This is my home now. You're right. I am terribly lonely; I've always felt out of place, not belonging. I've been in search of something, and I believe it is here...please...What did you give me to drink?" I asked.

"It'll wear off soon. So, Cyndi, do you feel like dancing?" he boldly asked me, standing me up and supporting me.

There was slow Bengali music playing in the main room of the restaurant that we heard in the back room where we were in together—alone. With him supporting me, we danced slowly... He put his arms around my waist and placed my hands on his shoulders. I felt him rubbing my waist, and he pushed me closer to him so there was barely any room between us. I smelled his cologne, and because I felt so dizzy, I rested my head on his chest.

He bent down to whisper in my ear, "This feels nice; I like the way you feel."

"You had someone drug me. Why did you do this?" I asked him, slurring my words, extremely annoyed.

"I'm not sure what you're talking about, Cyndi; if you're not feeling well...I can take you home." I could almost picture the corners of his mouth forming a devious smile.

My legs began to feel like jelly, and I needed more support from Vishnu as more of the cocktail kicked in. I did my best to keep myself as refined as possible without behaving too much like a louse in front of him—although it would have been his fault.

"I can't believe you did this to me." That was the last thing I remember saying to him before I ran out.

I ran until I found myself in the South Park Street Cemetery. I ran behind a gravesite and threw up until I felt better. I stumbled around and found a tree to lay under to sleep off some of the drug so that I could make it back to my hotel room—safely.

☽

10/30/1993

I feel like I haven't written in forever! Well, I am getting more involved with the girls and their families. Charita is quite the reader, as well as mathematician. I gave her Romeo and Juliet, and how she loves to act out the characters! She will have her whole family playing each character in the novel. She is very stingy with the character Juliet—she loves to only play Juliet and no one else. Her whole family once invited me over to their home to act out a scene from the book. By having her family act out the characters from the play, in turn she has been teaching her family English. I could see the grief, the happiness, and the romance in their faces as the scenes were acted out. I even invited the English missionaries over one evening to watch the scenes. Charita became nervous with a new crowd around her. I told her it would be OK.

While she was performing, an English missionary, Greta, walked over to me and took me by the arm. "Charita is very talented. Thank you for purchasing all of those books for her. You know, if she had the right sponsor, she could be sent over to England to study in our foreign exchange program. What age is she now?" Greta asked me.

"She is fifteen years of age," I said.

Greta nodded her head. "It seems like you taught her to her grade level on some subjects. If she had a giving sponsor, she could possibly be prepared for sophomore year in high school, getting ready for her junior prom. Come on. Open your pockets to her. Look at this place. A bright young lady such as herself deserves more," Greta said to me.

I looked around and couldn't help but agree with her. I remembered the first day I saw Charita come out of a brothel with a john. My heart tells me it was the day her purity was taken from her. She had tear stains all over her sari, and her eyes were bloodshot and red. She looked sore, and if my eyes did not betray me, there were blood stains on her skirt, dripping down to her sandals. With her hands quivering, she had given her mother the money from the john, and her mother had snatched the money out of her grasp. Her mother lightly patted her hair and walked away from her. She did not embrace her daughter or even show signs of empathy for her. I've never cared for her mother, even to this day.

I was there for her daughter. I had cleaned Charita up that day, and we talked about the books and stayed in the world of fairy tales, just the way she wanted it to be. I had held her and cradled her until I helped her to her bed, and she fell asleep. How I prayed she was dreaming of unicorns and fairy godmothers while she slept, as she needed to escape from her cold, harsh realities as often as she could. I shook my head, knowing Charita deserved more than this.

"How much are we talking for her education?" I asked Greta.

A gracious smile formed across Greta's face. "That depends... How deep are your pockets?"

This explains so much, Aisha thought. She saw Charita's sister Tarala walking with the john who allegedly treats her like gold. He saw her but kept holding Tarala's hand as they went into another building. *Maybe he is a kind man,* Aisha thought.

It was becoming dusk in West Bengal, and she noticed rats were beginning to appear on the street, eating scraps of food that they discovered. More men were starting to walk around the area. She saw a few in business suits and some in casual clothing. Since being in the district, she had not seen any men who behaved like consulate protection. Deciding it best not to worry about it, she read the next journal entry.

11/3/1993

I can't wait to hear how things went with Charita telling her family that I put up the money for her to study in England! I can't wait to see the joy on their faces! They have to be happy for her. She can go on to become a successful woman, possibly a teacher. I can see her studying in Oxford; oh, I am so happy for her! Every penny I gave her was worth it; although, it did set me back a little. Thank God for her family giving food to me. I spent so much money providing textbooks and sponsoring her that at times I do not have any money left to get a decent meal for myself. I've become these women on some levels: not knowing what I'm going to eat from day to day, appreciating the days when they met nice men who treated them well.

I'm spending less time at the hotel even though the paper pays for me to be there. That's mostly because I do not have any rupees at times to get a taxi ride there and have to wait until the next time I get paid from the paper. I keep my credit cards, work visa, and passport locked up in the hotel safe in my room on Sudder Street. The money I put up to sponsor Charita came from my 401(k) I had with the paper. On the days I really felt I needed a good shower, I muster up the strength to walk from Sonagachi up to Sudder Street.

Oh, these hot and humid days! People on the streets look at me funny. Some men even ask me how much in Hindi! If there is any saying I know in the Hindi language, it is, How much, I've heard it so often. I don't say anything and just walk on until I get to my hotel room and throw my body under the hot running water of the showerhead. I remember being in the hotel room at night crying. I feel torn: I could at any time leave Sonagachi, but why do I care so much for these women? I feel guilty enjoying simple pleasures like thorough showers and hotel dining. Vishnu, whom I have not seen since he had someone place something in my drink, was right. I am nothing but these women's false idol...But my heart loves to give, so that's why I give.

As I was helping a little boy named Daksha with a portrait he was drawing of me, Charita ran over to me, crying. I will never forget this day. As she sputtered something to me in Hindi, she grabbed me up, and we ran to the side of one of her sisters, who was lying in her bed. She was sweating feverishly. Her mother placed a cold, wet rag on her head. I touched her arm, trying to look in her eyes to see if I could place what her illness was. My hand being warm, she shook it away.

"She has chills," Charita said to me.

I remember Greta telling me one evening she worked for an English missionary clinic that specialized in treating STDs for the women in Sonagachi. "Stay here with your sister. I am going to get help," I said to Charita.

I ran as fast as I could run into different lecture groups I had spoken with here and there, until I found Greta. I pulled her away from a lecture on contraceptives she was giving some of the prostitutes. She turned her instructions over to a helper of hers.

"Greta, please come with me. It's Sati. She is sick; very ill," I said in between gasping for air from the running I did to get to her.

Greta looked at me as if she was preparing to have to report to Charita and her family the very worst.

Greta, myself, and three other missionaries got to the cot Sati was lying on; she was asleep—shivering. We all managed to get her on a makeshift gurney, and Greta and the others walked three blocks to a small clinic Greta's missionary had set up for emergencies such as this. Because I could not help in any way with diagnosing her problem, I waited with Charita's family in their home. We were very silent, skipping lunch and, later, dinner. It had to be twelve midnight when Greta finally came to their home. Charita and I both walked up to her, waiting for the results of what they could possibly diagnose.

"Your sister is very ill; she is showing signs of a flu-like disease. We need to take her to England before she suffers any further; there is no hospital here that will provide her proper care," Greta said, regretfully delivering the news.

Charita held her head and kneeled down with a shocked look in her eyes, shaking her head.

"Walk with me," Greta whispered in my ear. We walked a couple of feet away from Charita so that she was not in earshot. "Cyndi, we believe Sati is HIV-positive; she is exhibiting all of the symptoms: swollen lymph nodes, she has the chills, wakes up sweating, she has rashes on parts of her body and developed ulcers in her mouth. We don't think she has long. We must do something to get her to proper medical care," Greta informed me, looking over to Charita to make sure she did not walk over to us.

"I wish there was more I could do. I have given as much as I can...The money I put up to sponsor Charita is all I had left to give. I still have to live and be able to get back to the US...eventually," I said to Greta.

"Have they given you a date yet?" Greta asked me. I shook my head. She looked at me with a confused expression but returned the conversation back to Sati. "All I can do for her now is provide ibuprofen and keep her in clinic care. If you stumble into money anytime soon, let us know...because like I said, she does not have long..." Greta walked away.

I remember staying with Charita, her mother, and other sisters at the clinic until early the next day. I felt drained and tired along with them. We all went back to their home toward midday and got some sleep until the following day. I decided it would be best to not share with Charita what Greta told me; I figured I'd eventually find a way to help Sati.

When we all finally got up, we ate lunch in the alleyway as Charita acted out one of her favorite scenes from Romeo and Juliet for me. Just as she was about to recite another line, a john approached her, and they went inside a brothel. I continued to eat my food as her mother looked at me with disdain.

We continued to eat until she asked me in a gruff manner, "You done?"

I nodded my head as she snatched the plate from me and handed it over to another woman who was washing the dirty dishes.

Charita's mother got in my face and said, "Charita stay right here! She stay in Sonagachi. Her sister very ill. More money needed in family since Sati can't work. She stay here!" She jabbed her pointer finger in my face.

It took every ounce of good in me to not slap her finger out of my face. How selfish of her mother! I thought to myself. She turned around in disgust, spit in the street, and walked away.

☾

11/8/1993

I decided it would be best to give Charita and her family some space, in particular her mother. I checked on Sati every day, as she was looking weaker and weaker. Greta always reminded me she did not have long. I was feeling overwhelmed with guilt that I could not assist. I would have used the money I put up for Charita to go to England to study, but the English missionary organization gave me the runaround. When I called their head offices, they claimed they were not sure where the money went and regretted to inform me that they could not reimburse me for the funds. I felt defeated and did not know who to turn to. To keep positive, I continued to hold lectures with Dr. Jana's group, advocating healthy sex practices to the women and educating them on symptoms of contracting sexually transmitted diseases. I always courteously thanked Indian women who volunteered to translate for me during these seminars, as there was usually one in the crowd who knew English.

When I was not helping out with the seminars, I was latching onto another family—The Trivedi family of eight children: five girls and three boys. All were gifted and talented in their own right. Two of the females were amazing singers; all of the boys were exceptional in academics—particularly science. We had a few of the European missionaries tutor them on the periodic table, and they quickly absorbed the information.

"These boys are so smart; they could possibly discover the cure for deadly diseases. Imagine how they could help their people!" Greta would often say to me with her hand out, looking for cash.

I always agreed with her but had learned my lesson the first time. My bank account was from now on closed, but my heart always opened to the people. One day I had enough of Greta's cheesy verbal advertisements and turned her hand toward herself, asking her to provide financially. She raised her eyebrows as if I had insulted her, and she did not speak to me for three days! Hilarious! I thought.

Diwali, Festival of Lights
ज्योतिपर्व दीपावली

It began to drizzle and Aisha walked back into the makeshift temple, where some of the girls were learning traditional dances. Aisha got close to the light that was near the goddess Kamala to continue on to the next journal entry.

11/11/1993

It's time for Diwali, the festival of lights! All of the women a couple of days ago taught me traditional Hindu dances, and we all were decorated from head to toe in traditional saris. These women each had the most beautiful saris made out of the finest of materials that they specifically reserve for the festival of lights. We each got henna decorations up to our forearms. We placed red dye in our hair and in the middle of our eyebrows. The women dressed me in a red-colored sari and matching skirt decorated with orange designs. As the women adorned me in their traditional dress, I was given something—a box.

"This is from Vishnu," one of the young ladies said.

Not having seen Vishnu in weeks, I was shocked but opened the box. I pulled out three gold necklaces, and they looked like real gold. I placed them over my head and also took out a note that was inside of the box:

> Take a break from fighting crime to enjoy Diwali.
> —Vishnu

I smiled at the note and adornments.

Later in the evening, the red-light district was alive with celebration. There were smiles in all directions. Charita and I danced the night away. Before the festivities began, we stopped in to see Sati, whose eyes looked brighter, cheering us on for the festival of lights. Charita and I eventually parted ways once we got in the crowd.

Another woman tapped my shoulder. "Vishnu want to see you," the woman said. She had on a orange choli and a long, flowing, matching skirt. She was adorned with modest jewelry, compared to mine.

As she was walking in front of me, I tried to remember how I knew her face. Vishnu had talked about her to me; it was Elina. There were men with rifles standing in the doorway we walked through. Vishnu must be a very powerful man, I said to myself. Elina reluctantly showed me where Vishnu was and sent a rather envious look my way before leaving the room.

Vishnu was surrounded by females who were belly dancing in a circle around him. The table Vishnu was seated at had two lit candles and two dishes with fine Indian cuisine. I waited for the last woman to shimmy her way over to Vishnu's side of the table so I could finally sit down. He had on a cream-colored suit, with a gold ring on his ring finger.

"Hello." Vishnu spoke softly and calmly.

"Hey," I said back. I had nothing to say to him. I was waiting for him to apologize to me for slipping a Mickey in my drink. He just continued to stare. It figures. He is never going to apologize, I thought. I crossed my arms in front of my chest. "I'm assuming you called for me because you want me to return the necklaces. Well, here." I was about to take them off.

"No, that's not why! Do not take them off—they are yours to keep," Vishnu said. He placed a cigar to his mouth, and one of the women lit it for him. He puffed on the cigar for a little, looking me up and down. "You look festive for the occasion. I saw you dancing; you plan to dance for me later?" he said, flirting with me.

I smiled on the inside, but a thought occurred to me. "Vishnu, I have a request of you. I'm glad you called for me," I said to him.

"You have a request for me?" Vishnu said, raising one eyebrow. He instructed in Hindi for everyone to leave the room. "I want to hear this!" he said sternly.

"One of the women I've been staying with, Charita—you know her..." I said. Vishnu continued to stare at me. I noticed how his brown eyes appeared more reddish brown in the dim candlelight. He did not show signs of acknowledging Charita but kept staring at me. "Listen, Charita's sister Sati is ill. One of the missionaries thinks she contracted HIV. She needs to get treated in better facilities than what we can provide her here in Sonagachi, but I do not have the money to do this." I looked up to reveal watery eyes, in part due to the fact that I cared very deeply for Charita's family but also so that he saw how much it hurt me, since I knew he was developing feelings for me.

Vishnu kept a straight face and continued to smoke his cigar. "What else?" he asked.

I tried not to show it on my face, but I was amazed at how that did not faze him. "Well, it's the Trivedi family, with the five girls and three boys. All of these children are incredibly gifted; you should see them. I agree with the missionaries: the boys are geniuses when it comes to science, and the girls can sing like hummingbirds. We've talked to their parents already, and they are OK with the idea of them leaving Sonagachi to advance their talents. Again, this requires finances that I just do not have," I concluded, looking down. There was silence for a while between us as we heard laughter, music, and chanting in the background.

"I have something for you." Vishnu snapped his fingers, and a man with a camera came in. "I want you to sit over there." Vishnu pointed to an area of the room that was set up with a chair in front of a black backdrop and lighting equipment. "This is Rajani. I hired him to take your photo. I knew you'd look beautiful and wanted to remember this evening."

Vishnu began to speak in Hindi to Rajani, who positioned me the way he wanted to before taking the first photo. We carried on for a few minutes, and Vishnu stared as I changed pose after pose. I must have changed up to ten different poses, until I told Vishnu I had had enough. "I think you have plenty of photos of me to last you a while," I said to him, shooing the photographer away.

Vishnu translated for Rajani to leave the room and paid him. Vishnu and I walked back to the candlelit table and waited for the photographer to remove his equipment before speaking further.

"You have earned quite the reputation in Sonagachi. The women here—they feel they can trust you. There has never been an American who has gotten as close to the women as you have—they love you here. One of the photographs is going in the temple they created. You have become...their idol." Vishnu held out his hand to grab mine. He caressed my hand and kissed it. "Your requests are rather large. I know who Sati is, and I'm afraid I cannot help her." Vishnu put my hand down and inhaled his cigar. He exhaled and spoke. "I do not get involved financially with individual families in that way. It's a personal choice I've made. If I help one HIV victim, I'd have to help all of them. Some of the men that work for me involved themselves with Sati a couple of times, and each man told me she never once demanded a condom. If it wasn't for them having protection on their own, she wouldn't have provided any. She is known in the district to not protect herself—that is in part why she does so well financially for her family, but her ignorance may have caught up to her," Vishnu explained.

"Some men here will turn a female away if they even so much as suggest a condom! Why are you making this her fault?" I shrieked at him.

"She made her choices, kitten—if one man turns away because she uses protection, then there are plenty more who will oblige. All of the women in that family are beautiful! I am well loved here. Once my people find out that I helped Sati, I would be hated overnight. I don't get involved individually. I help through organizations only and give out trinkets here and there. Ahh, do you hear my men? They are throwing out some rupees now to the crowd. Hear them chant!" Vishnu said with a satisfied smile on his face.

I shook my head at him in disgust. And my familiar scowl, which he had seen when he met me, came back. "What about the eight children? Someone deserves a happy ending besides you!" I said to him. "Didn't someone help you to get where you are? What have you done to acquire so much money? You talk like you studied in England yourself. What makes you so special but the rest of your people deserve to suffer!" I spewed at him in disgust.

He looked at me, shocked that I had spoken the truth to him. "I'm a businessman. I was a child of Sonagachi who did study in England many years ago. I was put through school by a sponsoring English family. When I completed school, I took a job in England trading on the stock market. Like you, I thought it be a great idea to leave my ghetto behind, but I decided after a while to return home. England grew boring for me, as I was not as attracted to European women or the food or the climate. I came back to my people and now run the town. I give my people enough for them to love me but never take so much from me that I grow poor. I will never be poor again. I have been known to silently sponsor children every year here to study elsewhere, but eight children is asking a lot. A sacrifice is needed for this request. How bad do you want these children to be sponsored so they can move on from cruel circumstances?" Vishnu asked me, looking at me from the corner of his eyes, as his body was positioned facing sideways on his chair.

"Terribly. I want to say there was hope for some people here before I leave," I replied.

"Well, if you want hope for some, as you say, then you can't leave. If you are willing to trade their lives for yours, your wish will be granted," Vishnu said.

I was stunned. Does he mean me dying for this! Oh, hell no! That ain't happenin, I thought to myself. "What do you mean when you say sacrifice?" I asked him.

"You stay here...with me. You live here and be with me. I've wanted you, Cyndi, since I first laid eyes on you. You're lonely and there is no one for you to go back to in the States; you belong to me. You agree to exchange who you once were for those children, and your wish will be granted. But here's the thing: if you agree, then you can never go back to America. Like I said: you belong to me. Cyndi Jenkins will no longer exist; that person must be put to rest, and a new persona will be reborn. You are so pure and good-natured. Tonight you look exquisite...my black gold. You will be my Black Gold, my Lakshmi, my goddess." Vishnu took a sip of his drink that was in front of him. "Are you ready to eat?" he asked me, taking a bite of his food.

"Oh no, I'm not falling for that. I am not getting sick," I said to him, surprised to deny a request of his for the first time.

"There was something placed in your drink that night because I had to find out the truth from you. People come here from all over the world. Many have exploited our children to gain their own wealth. Some have been honest, but none have been as genuine as you. You really care about my people; the women here adore you. Please eat and enjoy Diwali," he said to me.

We ate in silence as his belly dancing women came back into the room. When I was done with my food, he requested that I join them in dancing for him and told every man to vacate the room, as I was only there for his enjoyment.

When early morning came, I was tired and ready to go back to my hotel. Vishnu had one of his men drive me to Sudder Street in one of his cars. We both sat in the backseat of the car.

"I haven't slept on my own bed in days. My back is killing me." I grabbed my upper back and rubbed it.

"You have proven to my people that you are one of them. Never feel guilty about taking care of yourself. Have you given thought to what I told you?" he said while placing his hand on the inner part of my thigh. My body grew warm from his intimate touch.

"I would have to leave everything I've ever known behind me? So that means taking on a new identity?" I asked him.

"Yes, that's right. Remember, you told me there was nothing in America for you anyway. I am helping you; you can be a goddess here. What is there to think about?" he said to me matter-of-factly.

"Well, for one thing, I have family back home. I've only known Cyndi as an identity. I have nothing else to identify with. Granted, it's not a luxurious life, but it's all I know," I said to Vishnu.

"I am offering you a chance of a lifetime. Do you know how many women wish they could be mine? And you're still confused," Vishnu said as the car stopped in front of my hotel.

I looked out to the street and thought of all the people who have touched me here, the purpose I have gained here, and how happy it would make me to help those children. "All right. I want to be with you." There, I had said it! And I meant it as well.

Vishnu removed his hand from my thigh and traced it slowly up my body, wrapping it around my shoulder. He whispered in my ear, "Then you come home with me tonight so we can properly consummate our union." He stroked my face.

I looked into his eyes, as they were hypnotic and dreamy. I turned my gaze to the hotel. I was tired of going to bed alone on a cot that hurt my back and living in a hotel room not even close to the size of a studio apartment's bedroom. "Let's go home," I said to him.

He drew my lips to his mouth and kissed me. He told his driver to leave the hotel, and we drove off into the night to our home.

BLACK GOLD
आबनूस सोना

$\mathcal{A}$isha placed the last journal entry to her heart and rocked herself back and forth. "I'm so happy for you, Cyndi," she said out loud. She noticed Charita standing a couple of paces away, smiling at her.

"Thanks for helping me to bed. You are so much like her. So, you're up to speed on her entries to you?" she asked Aisha.

Aisha nodded and the two headed out of the temple. "I can't wait until I get the next set," Aisha said, passing by some men catcalling to the both of them.

"I just saw Black Gold, actually. She was about to leave some new entries but noticed you in the temple...She does not think you're ready to meet her yet, I'm afraid. So she gave me the entries but told me to wait until next month to hand them to you," Charita said.

"Next month? Why? I am up to speed, like I told you! I just got to the romantic part—"

Aisha was cut off by Charita, who placed her pointer finger up to her mouth. "Remember, this is for you only—unless, of course, it involves me in some way." Both women laughed.

"About an entry involving you, Charita? How come I have not yet met your sister Sati?" Aisha asked.

The women got to Charita's room in her parents' building. None of her sisters were there, and they passed her mother and father before going into their home.

Charita grew quiet for a minute and patted the cot next to her for Aisha to sit on. "Sati passed away in 1999. She contracted HIV from one of the men out here. It was like a reality check for all of us. We all have been to Dr. Jana's lectures and the other missionaries who are here, but sometimes the information, I'll admit, goes in one ear and out the other. I know you're not a prostitute, Shadow, but have you always used protection with every man you've been with?" Charita asked.

Aisha was surprised by the forwardness of the question. "Well, to be honest, I have only had intercourse with one man ever in my life, and there were a few times we did not use protection," Aisha confessed.

"Exactly my point. Let me give you an example: Kamboja. I can view him as being far above the rest of my regulars. We've run out of condoms twice...and still had sex," she said to Aisha.

"Charita, it's different though. You don't know who Kamboja is with. Tonight he can be with you; tomorrow he can be with someone else," Aisha said, gesturing excitedly.

"What makes you think I can't say the same to you?" Charita challenged.

Aisha placed her hands on her hips, noticing Charita's boldness. "Well, for one, the relationship dynamic is different; we have more in common than intercourse," she explained.

"Kamboja likes to spend four hours with me every Monday. We talk, I cook for him, and we eat. There was one time he took me to Center Street, and we went to get dinner," Charita said as her eyes lit up. "Can you imagine? I've lived here my whole life and had never been on that side of town until he took me. That's where a lot of you tourists stay, I've noticed. Must be nice to sleep comfortably every evening," she said quietly, looking down.

"It's OK. I have learned so much from Black Gold and the experience she gained immersing herself into your lives. If Cyndi felt her touristy life was all that spectacular, she would not have grown to love you all the way she has and care for you," Aisha said. "Use protection, Charita, with everyone—including Kamboja. I was honest with you about my boyfriend because there is no need to lie. I've been with him for nine years, and even though we had a couple of slip-ups, we still use condoms to this day…that is, until we get married," Aisha said.

"Fantastic! When is that going to be?" Charita asked.

"Oh boy! That's another story not worth going into. So why does Black Gold want me to wait another month for her entries?" Aisha asked again, beginning to sprawl out onto the cot.

Charita followed suit and lay on her cot. "She wants you to get to know us better. She would like for you to get involved in the DMSC. Since she has been involved, many prostitutes work at the center as well. Black Gold really empowered us to help each other, and with Sati gone, most of us do in some way. I like to help out by teaching the children how to read English! I am good at basic math too. I have taught every child in Sonagachi addition, subtraction, multiplication, division, and fractions too!" Charita said, counting the math topics on her right hand.

"That's really good, Charita. I know Cyndi is proud of you. Say, Charita, seeing that Tarala is not here, do you think she would mind if I stay here tonight on her cot?" Aisha asked.

"Not at all. She won't be coming back until tomorrow. The guy she is with now likes to sleep with her afterward." Charita closed her eyes as she spoke.

Shortly after the women lay down, Aisha could hear Charita sleeping. She took out her cell phone that was hidden inside of her sari and text messaged Majid, explaining to him that she was staying with Nivritti that evening and would give him a call the following day. The truth was that she had not spoken with Nivritti in a while, but she felt she needed to lie to Majid so that he was not worried about her safety.

☾

A month passed and Aisha began to live a lifestyle similar to Black Gold when she was there. She volunteered at Dr. Jana's center, speaking about healthy sex practices to the women, and she also helped Charita with teaching the children in the district. She spent so much time there that the Trivedi family, who once opened their home to Black Gold because she sponsored their children, allowed Aisha a place to rest her head at night. Aisha, at times, did stay with Charita's family, but their home was always crowded. During her breaks from volunteering, she would walk a couple of blocks from Chittaranjan Avenue to a restaurant that had electric outlets. There she would charge her cell phone and call Majid.

One day when Aisha was assisting Mrs. Trivedi with the laundry at her home, Aisha inquired about her children. "Mrs. Trivedi, I noticed the photo of Black Gold with your children in your kitchen. How are they doing?" Aisha asked.

Mrs. Trivedi took from Aisha a folded sari and placed it in a basket. "The children are OK. They send me and their father some money each month. Our children wanted us to move out of here, but the money they provide is not enough for us to do so, and my husband and I refuse to be a burden to our children. We are happy they have moved on to do wonderful things. Not everyone in Sonagachi is into the drugs and prostitution here. My husband

and I did our best with the little money we make to keep our children from the bad elements. We did our best. But like in America, the media reports about a city being filled with crime…Well, not everyone that lives there is like that, right? Here in Sonagachi too. My three sons now live in England and are married, two of my daughters live in Mumbai, waiting for their big break into Bollywood films, and another lives in America—married. For my youngest two daughters, unfortunately, life was not as good to them. These two in particular were not the singers of the family and did not have great—what you all call, academic skill?" Mrs. Trivedi pronounced the last words slowly.

Aisha nodded her head, showing her she understood.

"When they got to England to study with their siblings, they did not do well behaviorally and socially. Had a lot of problems fitting in, so they came back to Sonagachi," she said. "My two girls lived with us for a period of time, and I warned them about getting involved in what goes on in the district. They ignored me and their father's warnings. They got involved with the wrong type of men, who got them addicted to drugs, and I had to bury my two youngest daughters four years ago." Mrs. Trivedi's voice grew weak, as she was holding back tears.

Aisha stopped removing the clothes from the line outside to help Mrs. Trivedi sit down on a wooden stool. "I'm sorry I brought it up. I just heard that Black Gold sponsored your children, and I was hoping there was a happy story for all eight of them," Aisha responded.

"Shadow, my dear, just like Black Gold, you both wish for happy endings for everyone. That's sweet, but life doesn't work that way," Mrs. Trivedi said, straining to get off the stool to continue folding the clothes. "You think my family is the only one who has suffered? You both have no idea. I am thankful for six of my children doing well; two of them did not, but they made terrible choices in their lives. To see my beautiful daughters transition from looking alive and healthy to becoming drug abusers...My husband and I were thankful to put them to rest. They no longer suffer, and I no longer worry—it's the pain of losing them that way that makes me cry." Mrs. Trivedi managed a smile. "The day our children were sent to England to study was the last day I saw Black Gold. Yes, she is respected here and loved by many, but if I were to see her again, I would ask her if she still feels she made the best choice for herself." Mrs. Trivedi paused.

"What do you mean?" Aisha asked her.

"She is locked up in Hari Vishnu's castle! Yes, she gets bestowed with all of the riches of the world, but that woman lost the only life she knew! How selfish of Vishnu to banish her from her own family forever. They all think she is dead. You would think a woman like her would grow a conscience after a while and want to get in touch with them. Her sacrifice to most of us out here did not make any sense, but we keep quiet out of respect for her selfless acts of kindness she's made, and, also, Vishnu is a very powerful man! You don't cross him—ever! But at times we bring them up and talk about their interesting companionship." Mrs. Trivedi rolled her eyes. "The story is that he loved her at first sight. You know, Vishnu's men are from Sonagachi too, and after meeting Black Gold, Vishnu would speak of her so much to them that their ears would ring of her name all day—every day," Mrs. Trivedi said. "He had other women during the time he flirted with Black Gold, but they all told the district he would speak Black Gold's name in the heat of the moment. Isn't that crazy!" Mrs. Trivedi chuckled.

All Aisha did was listen. She was curious to hear what the people of the district really thought of Vishnu and Cyndi's relationship.

"The story continues that once she told him she would be his forever, he no longer wanted any woman in the district and no longer even so much as looked at one with desire. He really only has eyes for Black Gold," Mrs. Trivedi concluded, placing a cigarette in her mouth and lighting it.

Aisha hadn't smoked since she left America, and once she smelled the nicotine, her eyes glimmered and a smile formed on her face. Mrs. Trivedi noticed Aisha's reaction and gave her a cigarette and the lighter.

"Their story sounds like a fairy tale," Aisha said, blowing the smoke out of her mouth.

Mrs. Trivedi nodded her head and exhaled smoke from her mouth as well. "Shadow, my dear, I am an old woman—seen lots of things here. You know, my mother used to watch over Vishnu when he was around six years of age. He was always a very smart boy. A true leader never did anything that other people tried to pressure him into. Before Dr. Jana started his organization, the British were here. We'd see some who helped our children and some who exploited them. Vishnu was very lucky. By ten years of age, he left Sonagachi to study in England. His parents were very poor. His mother was a prostitute, and his father pimped his mother. They both were killed when he was seven years old. We never saw that boy cry once for his parents; he kept it all bottled up. When the missionaries met him, they could not take advantage of him the way they could other children. He was always bigger and taller than most children his age. By ten years old, before he left for England, he was built like a grown man. The English missionaries needed to prove to their people back home, give evidence that they were providing help to Sonagachi and not taking advantage of the people—they began to sponsor our children to go to England for school.

"Vishnu was one of the first to go over to study. He did exceptionally well but decided to come back. He owns offices in the business district and funds a lot of the missionaries in Sonagachi. When he got back from England, he could pick and choose any woman he wanted. My belief is that these women reminded him too much of his mother—a prostitute. And any woman who is in that life cannot be faithful to any man. A woman who would sell her body to a man would sell anything! No man could ever marry a woman like that. He confided in my mother once when she would watch over him. This six-year-old boy told my mom he saw his mother involved with men other than his father and did not understand why. At his young age, he saw a lot, and to see his mother in that way I'm sure was shocking to him," Mrs. Trivedi said. "Fast-forwarding the story, he comes back from England a grown man, starts businesses on Sudder Street and a few around here. Years pass and finally he meets his true love—Black Gold. The story persists that for a while he investigated her—he was not sure of her intentions. Was she just another prostitute trafficked from another country? Did she work for the consulate? He paid so many people off to investigate her. Once she seemed to be the person she said she was, he made it his plan to make her his own—forever. He is very controlling of her to this day. When Black Gold leaves his fortress, she does not go anywhere unless protected by his men. Can you imagine living like that?" Mrs. Trivedi said.

Aisha could not help but to think there was some level of envy that Mrs. Trivedi had for Cyndi and decided on an impartial comment to share. "I am not sure what to make of their relationship, but possibly Black Gold is content with how she is cared for. Perhaps their union was meant to be," Aisha said, smoking her cigarette.

Out of the corner of her eye, Mrs. Trivedi gave a repulsive look to Aisha and exhaled her cigarette. "They are the fairy tale story of the red-light district. We all know and tell our children their story—they are the Romeo and Juliet of our dwellings. Bet you didn't think there could be a story like this created from the slums." Mrs. Trivedi threw her cigarette in a puddle on the street and took the basket of folded clothes into her home.

*D*ecember finally came. During the month of November and the first two weeks of December, Aisha spent all of her time in Sonagachi. She grew to care for the families and the women in the district who all told her varying stories of Vishnu and Black Gold's relationship. The stories got more and more amusing and mystical depending on whom she spoke to. Judging from the journals she received, which the women were not aware of (except for Charita), she thought the story that was closest to truth was the very first one she had heard from Mrs. Trivedi. Charita had still not provided the remaining Black Gold journal entries.

Aisha knew in her last week of being in West Bengal that she had better get started on her assignment. She took a break from the DMSC to stay in the business district at her hotel and write about Black Gold.

She looked at her blank laptop screen. "What in the hell do I write?" Aisha said to herself. Under no circumstances was she going to reveal that Cyndi was still alive, but she did come to India to specifically write about this woman. "How can I keep my job at the *Hartford Journal* but still respect Cyndi and Vishnu's relationship?" Aisha said. She picked at her fingernails until she came up with a bright idea. "Got it. Thanks for the variations of the stories, ladies. It's time to put them into print. I'll just blend the stories that the women of Sonagachi shared with me of Black Gold and Vishnu's life, but I'll make sure Cyndi has a tragic ending, like Romeo and Juliet!" Aisha said, beginning to type...

*T*hree hours of writing passed, and Aisha met up with Nivritti at the Blue Sky Café on Sudder Street. This was their initial meeting since the first time Aisha went to the red-light district. Nivritti was already sitting down at a table near the window when Aisha walked in.

"Shadow, long time. Good to know you are still alive!" she said sarcastically.

"Of course. Sorry for not sending text messages every evening, but I figured I was still being watched," Aisha said, looking at the menu.

"Well, yes. I was just joking. Our men have known where you are, but they cannot go as far into the district either—something about the high-power boss Vishnu who has a lot of influence with many government organizations. Even some people in the consulate are on his payroll! His men never cross him! I never told you this because I did not want you to worry. They arranged with Vishnu to only watch you for small periods of time. Whenever there were large crowds of people in the district, they were there protecting you. But from what they reported to me over the weeks, you must have spent lot of evenings there alone, because they never saw you catch a taxi on Chittaranjan Avenue," Nivritti said in a surprised manner.

Aisha nodded her head. "The people in that area are poor, not stupid. If you want information from them, you have to earn their trust, and by staying there for only a couple of hours a day, I would not have gained their trust," Aisha finished before speaking to a waitress.

Nivritti stared at Aisha for a while and finally spoke. "You look different. You look like you've become more mature—if that's the correct word to use. I can tell this assignment has opened your eyes to a whole new world. I'm proud of you, Shadow. The first day I took you to Sonagachi, I must admit, I was not sure that you'd make it! You were not very street smart and stuck out like a sore thumb, but you have a different look about you. You've grown from this experience, so I see. Good for you." Nivritti was picking at her fruit salad as she spoke. "But in this reunion, I am going to still need to get down to business with you. Your boss will need your paper finalized by this Saturday and sent to him by e-mail. You are also to leave all physical materials and documents with me that you received from the district. We are going to go by good faith that you are truly providing to us *all* information that was given to you by the women, since I have been informed that this assignment makes or breaks your career with the paper. So I'm sure you will cooperate," Nivritti said, folding her hands.

Aisha was not surprised by Nivritti's remarks and finally realized why Charita did not allow her access to the red-light district. "Sure. I am going to cooperate and provide the information that tells the *mystical* story," Aisha said, a playful smile forming on her face.

On Wednesday evening in her last week of staying in Sonagachi, Aisha went back to the district to have dinner with Charita and her family. She helped prepare the Bengali food, and they were surprised she knew how to make a traditional Bengali dish.

After they ate, shared stories, and washed dishes, Charita whispered in Aisha's ear, "Let's go to my room. I have something to share with you." Aisha followed Charita into her room. Once they got there, Charita spoke in a low voice. "Close the door." They both sat on Charita's cot. Charita smiled at Aisha and removed two pages from underneath her worn mattress. "So this is your last week in Sonagachi. The time flew by; you made an impact, like Black Gold did. She told me she has one entry left for you and that you'll get it from her, sort of..." Charita said, brushing lint off her cot.

"Why did it take so long?" Aisha asked, looking down at the journal entries, feeling like she had a precious possession in her hand.

"You had to earn her respect first. You rested here, helped the people here, and grew as a person—like she did. She's been watching you, and she is very proud of your development," Charita said, smiling. "Shadow, listen—when you go back home, you are not to tell the people there she is alive; you must respect this request from her. Trust me: you do not want to cross her. Make something up about her disappearance, but under no circumstances should you tell anyone there she is still alive," Charita said, looking in Aisha's eyes. "Do you plan on staying tonight?" Charita asked Aisha.

"Yeah, I would like that. It's Wednesday. Is Tarala with her prince?" Aisha asked jokingly.

"You know it. My sister is waiting for him to rescue her from here. We all have had a chance to get other types of employment, but this place has pulled us in, and we can't get out," Charita replied.

"You don't want to get out, Charita, but I pray for you all every day. When I go home, there will not be a day that I forget what I've learned here and who I've helped. You women are fantastic, and I would love to hear how one day you all did move on to better circumstances," Aisha replied, lying on Tarala's cot.

"Sure, Shadow. Thanks for never judging us. Sleep well." Charita rolled over to face the wall in her room. "You're reading the journal entries tonight?" Charita asked after a while.

Aisha unfolded the journal entries and laughingly replied, "Yes, I could not wait."

"Good. Please come back on Friday at noon, the day before you leave. Lakshmi wants you to bring all the journal entries she provided you and come alone. She will meet you on Sidon Avenue, at the tallest high-rise building of our district," Charita said.

There was silence for a moment between them as Aisha listened to the noises coming from outside. "I have a question, Charita. How come Cyndi's name is Black Gold but also Lakshmi?"

"I believe these last few entries will tell you everything you need to know. You're almost at the end of her story," Charita said, closing her eyes.

12/2/93

I can't believe this happened to me, of all people me! The day I sacrificed Cyndi Jenkins was the day I became reborn. Cyndi was floating through life, not sure what she should do next, being pushed around and feeling like she only existed but never lived. I felt sorry for Cyndi—myself. I knew I deserved more and had faith that something better was waiting for me. I had to believe I deserved it. I'd dream often, envisioning myself driving at night, only seeing as far as the headlights on my car allowed me to see but knowing I'd get to my fantasy destination...eventually.

Vishnu owns a four-bedroom home in a residential part of Kolkata known as Jadavpur. The home is gorgeous! We have twenty-four-hour security and palm trees shading the front of our home. The backyard is landscaped to perfection, and we have a maid and butler! I never thought in my life I would be given such gifts! When we arrived at our home the night I made the pact with Vishnu, I knew I made the right decision. Vishnu is the most romantic man I've ever met, as well as the best lover I've ever had. The first three days we were together, we never left our bedroom! Vishnu rescheduled all of his meetings in the business district, and I was missing in action from Sonagachi for the three days we were together.

I found out that Vishnu owns a community bank in Kolkata in the business district and also three restaurants, including the one we first spoke in near Chittaranjan Avenue! No wonder he knew the menu so well. He had a couple of his men go into the hotel room I stayed at on Sudder Street and remove every item I brought. On our third day of celebrating our union, we both watched my past life's belongings get torched in our backyard. I won't write how we were able to get me a new identity—some things are better left unwritten—but I will write that anything is possible when you have the right connections and capital to do so.

Today Vishnu gave me my ID card with my new name: Lakshmi Vishnu. He kissed me on my left shoulder and spoke in my ear, "Lakshmi is the goddess of wealth and prosperity: spiritually and materially. You've proven that you deserve all the riches I can acquire for us in the world for what you've done for my people—they are your people now too. Together we bring them balance. Rule with me, my dearest love."

I cannot resist this man and happily accepted my new identity. I think of my family often. I miss them very much, but I will never betray my husband. He saved me from just existing in this world. I am now living.

We are heading to Uttar Pradesh, not too far from New Delhi, for a weekend trip! Imagine me, Cyndi Jenkins—hmph, excuse me, Lakshmi Vishnu—heading to Uttar Pradesh for a weekend trip because I have the money and feel like it! I love my life! Hari wants me to experience the Taj Mahal with him. That's right! Not see it, but experience it! After all, the architecture was constructed from the inspiration of the most beautiful love story ever told in India...well, ranked second to ours, of course!

12/12/93

We got back last week from Uttar Pradesh, and Hari surprised me by flying a few of his family members and friends out there for our marriage ceremony. We became legally married not too long after we moved in together but did not hold a ceremony until our trip to Uttar Pradesh. I owe this man my life! I have never been so happy and felt so loved. I no longer work but continue to volunteer my time in the district, as he knows this provides great joy to me. Vishnu at first did not want me to resume my undertaking but felt better about it once he paid for me to be guarded with security. I have encouraged many of the young women to protect themselves and to also teach each other the importance of healthy practices. I am a legend in the red-light district and the beloved wife of Vishnu—my life could not get any better!

It was twelve noon on Friday, and as instructed, Aisha had in her hand all the journal entries and arrived at the district alone. She had her suitcases packed and ready to go at her hotel. The only thing left for her to do was complete her paper before handing it in to the consulate and e-mailing it to Larry. As Aisha walked toward Chittaranjan Avenue, she saw Charita. Charita was dressed in an all-white sari and smiled at Aisha.

"She's waiting for you; just continue to walk toward the high-rise building. I will wait for you right here," Charita said, placing her hand on Aisha's shoulders.

Aisha smiled and nervously walked toward Sidon Avenue. As Aisha got to the high-rise building, she noticed how windy the day was and folded her arms across her chest, looking around to see if a woman was coming toward her. She waited for what felt close to fifteen minutes. Growing impatient, she was about to turn back around, when a man with an artillery weapon strapped across his chest pushed his rifle toward his back and handed Aisha a piece of paper folded the exact same way as the other journal entries. Written on the fold was: *For Shadow*.

The man said, "Here you go, Ms. Reign. Mrs. Vishnu is running late. She apologizes for her tardiness and wants you to read this." With that, the man walked away and returned to his post at the entranceway of the building.

Aisha unfolded the last entry but noticed it read more like a letter:

> Dear Shadow:
>
> This is my last journal entry; there is no more to share. You now have the mystical story that Kolkata, my people, kept from the world. This story is going to reap huge rewards for you; you will be validated with this story and respected by your colleagues. Take heed of two of the people you work with. One person's first initial is K, the other is J. They do not care for you and will try to bring you down; one of them acts close to you to find things out about you for other people in the office, especially for the person whose first initial is J.
>
> To be honest with you, the paper I worked for has sent over the years many people here to find me. I never gave anyone the time of day—that is, until I saw you. I entertained you perhaps because of our resemblance in features. You were chosen to get this story because you have a genuine spirit, quite childlike in that it is so honest and transparent. Unlike the people at your job, you possess an extraordinary empathy for those who are the underdog; you like to truly help people and dislike injustice.

There are a group of people who need your help once you get back. The gods told me you are to go back and protect some people you work with; they told me you would know what that means. You are the only one who can do that, because no one else will have the influence or, much less, care to.

I am NOT going back to the US; there is nothing there for me. This is my home, and this is my final resting place. I am a much-exalted person in Kolkata. Read the next sentence very carefully and slowly to understand: Aisha (yeah, I always knew your real name), if you tell the people back in America that I am still alive, all the prosperity you will receive from this story will come to a tragic end, and I will find out.

Charita will see you out of the district. You are not to come back here. You became very close to my people and cared for them the way I did—thank you. Charita will take this letter from you, since this letter is not needed for your story back home, along with the journal entries dated 11/11/93, 12/2/93, and 12/12/93. You are exceptional and brave...Enjoy the rest of your life.

You have a strapping consort who would do anything for you. When you get back to the US, he will finally give you what you've patiently waited for.
Lakshmi

Once Aisha finished reading the letter, she looked up to the sky and noticed a woman looking directly at her from a window in the tallest high-rise building in the district. Aisha changed her stare to look directly across from her. She now saw ten men with artillery weapons who were stationed outside of that building.

Bringing her stare back up to the window, Aisha felt a chill go down her spine, looking into the woman's mysterious eyes, seeing how similar this woman's features looked to hers although she was older now. The woman was adorned with gold necklaces and a gold sari.

Behind this woman was a tall man who embraced her by the shoulders and looked out of the window. The man had on sunglasses and was fair complexioned with Asiatic features. Before the mysterious woman turned in the direction he was directing her to go, she nodded her head toward Aisha and then left the window.

Aisha couldn't believe that she merely gestured a hello and good-bye to the woman she came so far on a journey to find. She stood there for a second, taking her experience in while looking down at the pavement. She looked back again, and this time no one was there! The men with artillery weapons were gone, and she did not see a trace of Vishnu and Lakshmi.

Perhaps I've been standing here too long and just daydreamed? No, that can't be correct or I would not have received this letter. An eerie feeling passed through Aisha's body as she turned away.

She noticed a torn poster stuck on a building; the words were written in English as well as Hindi. There was tape covering some of the letters in the English portion of the word, only revealing *EVE*. She wiped away the tape and discovered the full word read *BELIEVE*. She removed the poster, folded it into her change purse, and continued walking.

"My lips are sealed, Cyndi," Aisha said to herself. In taking her final walk through the district, she longingly stared at the very last images and people she would never be able to see again.

Charita was standing at the end of Chittaranjan Avenue, where Aisha's journey first began. Aisha held out the final letter and journal entries for Charita to take from her hand. Charita shuffled through every entry, taking out the ones Cyndi had instructed, and returned the rest to Aisha.

"How come Cyndi did not want to meet me?" Aisha asked Charita softly.

"How can you meet someone who no longer exists?" Charita whispered back, smiling.

No further words were exchanged between the two of them, as everything was explained with their facial expressions. Aisha looked back once more before walking away from the red-light district—forever.

Assignment Completed
नयित कार्य पूरा हो गया

On Saturday morning Aisha e-mailed Larry her article of Black Gold and also made copies of the journal entries Lakshmi allowed her to keep. She decided it best give the copies to the consulate and to keep the originals for herself.

"It's funny how I feel so close to someone that I never really met," Aisha said to herself, placing all the documents in a folder to provide the consulate.

As she checked out at the front desk of the Broadway Hotel, Nivritti patted her on the shoulder. "Hey, Shadow. The *Hartford Journal* preferred that I meet you in the hotel lobby here so that they do not have to pay for additional fare for you to go from the consulate to the airport," she said.

Aisha smiled and took out the folder and handed it to Nivritti.

"Ahh, yes! Let's see what you have for us." Nivritti shuffled through the documents. "What is this? Copies of diary entries?" she asked mockingly.

"Well, you may call it that, but I prefer to use the term *journal entries*," Aisha said, folding her arms in front of her chest.

"So this means you all met, I'm guessing," Nivritti said.

"I never met her. From what I was told by everyone in the district, she is no longer alive. We found the journal entries in a temple the ladies created," Aisha explained.

"So if these journal entries, as you call them, were found, that means Cyndi, Black Gold—whatever she gets called now—lost them?" Nivritti asked, looking confused.

"We believe so. I was learning how to belly dance from Charita and her family one evening. And we were having such a great time messing around that we accidentally knocked over an idol, and underneath it were Black Gold's journal pages. She must have had them there for years, and no one noticed them," Aisha replied, loving how the lie rolled off her tongue so easily.

"Hindus wouldn't touch them! Perhaps she placed them there for luck, and we have so much respect for our gods we would never bother them. I'm sure Charita and her family prayed after you all knocked the statue over, right?" Nivritti said, looking serious.

"Of course we did." Aisha nodded her head.

"Good. Like I said to you a while ago, you do not want to mess with the gods."

"So I've been told by others," Aisha said, remembering Lakshmi's last entry.

Nivritti continued to shuffle through the folder, when she noticed a poster folded in fours. She opened it up. "*Believe*—was this also found underneath the statue?" Nivritti asked edgily.

"No, but I found it in the district, and you all specifically wanted every document from there," Aisha said, shaking her pointer finger at Nivritti in a mocking manner.

"You can have that back. You're funny, Shadow, taking us literally and all." She handed the poster back to Aisha. "Well, my dear, anything else I need to know, be aware of?" Nivritti asked.

The two of them went down the steps of the hotel to a taxi. Aisha rolled her bags over to the driver, who began placing them into his trunk. "You were right, Nivritti. I definitely have grown and changed from the person I used to be; this was an experience of a lifetime. Once my article is edited and printed in our papers, I will send you a soft copy by e-mail. Thanks for the tour of the business district."

Nivritti and Aisha shook hands. Aisha got in the backseat of the taxi and waved good-bye to Nivritti.

☾

Majid brought Aisha's two suitcases up the flight of stairs. Aisha walked into their condo before Majid did and went into their bedroom in a brisk fashion. As Majid entered their bedroom, rolling in her suitcases, he noticed that Aisha had not changed out of her black *khimar,* but she had turned it into a *niqāb* covering her entire face with the exception of her eyes; her legs were bare and crossed on the bed. She wore a low-rise black thong that revealed her gold belly necklace that hung low on her midriff.

"Look at you...Why did you not finish removing the khimar?" Majid asked her, inching closer, caressing her legs.

Aisha responded, "All is mystery; but he is a slave who will not struggle to penetrate the dark veil." She placed his hands on her *khimar* to help him remove it.

"Mmm, hmm, turning literary quotes into foreplay. Now I know why I picked a woman with an English degree to be my wife—that's right: I said it. Isha, I missed you so much, and I want you to be my wife." He removed his hand from her grasp and slipped a stunning one-carat diamond ring on her left ring finger. "I've had the ring for a couple of months now and wanted to wait for the perfect moment. I'd say right now—the way you look and the way I feel with having you back home—this is the perfect moment."

He picked her up to place her comfortably on their pillows. As he was looking down at her, he noticed how her body had a warm, brown glow to it. His eyes wandered from her belly necklace to the *niqāb* inspired look covering her chest up to her head, only revealing her cat-shaped eyes. He crawled on top of the bed, right above her body, and continued to take in the enticing scene below him.

"You're so stunning, every inch of you." He started at her feet, massaging his hands up to her thong, and began to remove it slowly, then tossed it down to the floor. He removed his jeans, boxers, and shirt. Majid's stare was intense and carnal. "Who said that quote now?" Majid asked, rubbing Aisha's legs.

"Mmm, Benjamin Disraeli, honey," Aisha said flirtatiously.

"There you go; my man knows what he's talking about." Majid grabbed both of Aisha's legs and pulled them down to him. "Now, this may hurt a bit. Disraeli is right: I have been a slave of my own thoughts for three months because I could not penetrate." He slowly parted her legs. "That is, penetrate your dark veil." He entered Aisha slowly as she let out a satisfied moan...

Aisha returned to work two days after she got back to the United States. Sitting at her desk, she played with the Rubik's Cube.

"Hey, girl!" Kelsey ran into her cube. "So...Tell me! I've got to know everything." Kelsey crossed her legs and had an inquisitive smile on her face.

Aisha paused, remembering what Lakshmi shared with her about Kelsey. "It was an unforgettable experience. I wrote the most mystical story readers of our paper will be sure to love,"

Aisha said, clicking with her mouse to get to another web page on her computer screen.

"And the best part is that it's a true story. So what is this Cyndi Jenkins like? Is she, like, thinking that she's Indian or something now?" Kelsey said with a Valley girl voice, laughing.

Aisha squint her eyes at Kelsey and thought to herself, *Well, Cyndi Jenkins looks more like the people over there than you do. That's why the paper sent me over there: to complete what Lydia couldn't years ago.* Aisha replied to Kelsey, "I don't know; I never met her." Aisha checked her e-mails and saw that Larry wanted her in his office ASAP.

"You didn't meet her, but that's why you were sent there. So does that mean that you failed the assignment?" Kelsey asked.

Aisha noticed that she had sort of a smirk on her face as she said that. *You were right, Lakshmi,* Aisha thought. "Kelsey, I bet one of your favorite quotes is, 'Keep your friends close, but keep your enemies even closer,' right?" Aisha asked, turning around for the first time to look Kelsey in the eyes.

Kelsey had a confused expression. "What are you talking about, girl?" Kelsey asked, laughing uncomfortably.

"Hmm, thought so. To answer your question: I wouldn't say I failed the assignment, but I guess I'll know after speaking to Larry—he wants me in his office pronto." Aisha got up and left her cubicle.

Kelsey walked closely behind her before turning right to walk down the next aisle over. "OK, girl. Tell me everything Larry says to you!" Kelsey yelled back.

Whatever, Aisha thought and replied back to Kelsey in a phony tone of voice, saying, "OK, girl!"

Aisha knocked on Larry's office door, and he immediately gestured with his hands for her to come in.

"I read over your story, Benson, and I must say...good job! It was written well. Julia Weathers and the board were quite entertained and amazed by the story. Our paper is flying off the shelves in cafés and grocery stores. I can't believe this story is real," Larry said.

"It's unbelievable!" Aisha responded, smiling.

"So, Cyndi Jenkins was not a prostitute then, huh? And the natives don't know how she died?" Larry asked.

"Correct. Cyndi was not a prostitute; she was a humanitarian. There is a lot of speculation surrounding her death. But the good she did is told like an urban legend throughout the red-light district. I can tell you honestly that Cyndi Jenkins is deceased, and Black Gold will forever be the name the people know her as, and her spirit lives on through them," Aisha said.

"Ha! Excerpt taken from 'Lost Journals of Black Gold,' quoting your article, I see. Benson, this is brilliant! I must say, I was rooting for you! You saved your job. Too bad I can't say that for the rest of them..." Larry said, holding a copy of Aisha's article in his hands.

"Umm, about that, sir. I wanted to speak with you. You know the paper's rankings are coming out tomorrow, and let's say that we are ranked higher for this current year. I believe it serves no purpose to let go of all of *my people*—I mean, *my work colleagues* who were on the list to be laid off," Aisha said confidently.

Larry rubbed his chin. "You've got a point, Benson. I'll speak about that with Julia, and we'll see," Larry said, placing the article down before shuffling papers on his desk.

Aisha noticed a document that had as the title, Journalism Assignments: Brazil, Ghana, and South Africa. "So you're sending other journalists to another country?" Aisha inquired.

"Well, that depends...meaning that it depends on you. You did a wonderful job, Benson, and I was going to wait later in the week, but since you're here now, I'll discuss it briefly with you. A journalist can choose from any of these three places; they all have a distinct commonality. They're considered newly industrialized nations and have lots of interesting stories to be written about. Our board thinks from now you should on get first dibs on these international assignments—I think I found a niche for you, Benson!" Larry said, excited for Aisha.

"Wow, that's great! What about Jared, though? I thought this was his forte," Aisha said.

"Not your concern. Now this assignment will be postponed for a while, but what do you say?" Larry asked, lifting the document up in the air.

Aisha thought about it for a second. "I say...let the gods decide." Aisha took the paper from Larry's hands and positioned it on the desk. She closed her eyes with her right hand and placed her left hand on the document. "Eenie, meenie, minie, mo!" Aisha's left pointer finger stopped on one of the countries.

"Hmm, that's an interesting one," Larry noted, looking down at what she picked.

Aisha opened her eyes and saw where her finger rested. "South Africa it is!"

About the Author
लेखक के बारे में

Samantha Perkins is a neuromuscular therapist and owner of Refuge of Therapeutic Healing and Wellness LLC in Georgia. Author of *Seduction* and the newly released *Lost Journals of Black Gold, Shadow Reign Chronicles Vol. 1*, Perkins is in the process of writing sequels for both. Perkins currently resides in Atlanta with her fiancé and Yorkshire terrier. For more information regarding her health and wellness practice, visit www.refugeofhealing.com.

Made in the USA
Charleston, SC
26 October 2014